D0933880

Other Books by
Natalie Savage Carlson

CARNIVAL IN PARIS

A PET FOR THE ORPHELINES

A BROTHER FOR THE ORPHELINES

THE FAMILY UNDER THE BRIDGE

THE HAPPY ORPHELINE

SASHES RED AND BLUE

THE SONG OF THE LOP-EARED MULE

THE TALKING CAT

THE TOMAHAWK FAMILY

WINGS AGAINST THE WIND

Jean-Claude's Island

Jean-Claude's Island

by Natalie Savage Carlson

Pictures by Nancy Ekholm Burkert

HARPER & ROW, PUBLISHERS, NEW YORK, EVANSTON, AND LONDON

JEAN-CLAUDE'S ISLAND

Printed in the United States of America.

For information address
Harper & Row, Publishers, Incorporated,
49 East 33rd Street, New York 16, N. Y.

Library of Congress Catalog Card Number: 63-8472

For my niece
Anastasia Craig Steere

Jean-Claude's Island

CHAPTER ONE

As far back as the history of Canada goes, the white geese have visited the St. Lawrence Valley in the spring and in the fall.

Some years ago a small boy named Jean-Claude Plouffe lived on an island in the river. One spring morning he drove his grandfather to the eastern shore to gather driftwood and whatever treasures the salty tide from the sea had been able to push through the river current that struggled against it.

Jean-Claude was disappointed because other than driftwood, all he found was a broken bottle and a shred of fishnet. But as their two-wheeled cart neared the tidal flats, a wonderful sight appeared in the sky. The white geese were coming toward the island. They were coming like a snow-storm blown across the channel.

His grandfather quickly tied the horse to a tree, then tried to catch up with Jean-Claude, who was racing for the tidal flats that attracted so many shore birds.

The wild geese came in one great, white flock. Soon they whitened the flats and their strange cries filled the valley.

"Pepère," said Jean-Claude, "the Boulets have geese but they do not fly. I think wild geese belong to the good God so that is why they can go up into the sky where He is."

"Ah, you are full of ideas, my little goodman," said Pepère, brushing the gray lynx whiskers below his wrinkled cheeks. "Your big brother Michel is trustworthy and your big sister Gabie is a perfect little *maman,* but you are the one with the well-made head."

Jean-Claude solemnly felt his curly black head. His eyes were dark, too, and he had a little crooked smile as if he wasn't sure of what was funny and what was not.

He and Pepère watched the geese hungrily feeding on the sedge grasses of the tide-washed flats. Their shrill cries sounded like the barking of many dogs.

"And now that we have properly welcomed the geese,"

said Pepère, "I must get back to my mill."

Pepère was a miller. His windmill on the bank of the river was one of the last in use. Let the people on the mainland eat store-bought bread that would only make them fat and lazy. Pepère's wind-ground flour made bread that built bone and muscle for the islanders.

"Pepère, where are the geese going?" asked Jean-Claude, because he knew that they would not stay for long.

"They are on their way to their nesting grounds in the Arctic," replied his grandfather. "They have spent the winter far south in the United States. They are like your grandmother. They do not belong here."

"But Memère stays here with us," said Jean-Claude.

"It is only because she has no wings to take her away," joked Pepère, but his words worried the boy.

Way back in the days when Pepère had been a sailor, he had brought Memère back from the Ile de Ré off the coast of France. He had brought her as his wife, and now she had lived most of her life on the little island in Canada. But she never stopped longing for her own island across the sea. "My island," she called it, and she spoke of the island in the St. Lawrence as "your island."

Pepère put his pipe back in his mouth and pulled at the boy's shoulder. Jean-Claude turned to follow his grandfather back to the cart, but he gave one last look over his shoulder before he climbed into it.

"Come," urged Pepère. "Your maman will be wondering what has happened to you."

Jean-Claude lowered his head. Every time Maman spanked him, he packed his nightshirt into his wagon and went to live with his grandparents in their house across the road. Of course he only lived with them for a few hours —just long enough to give Maman time to be sorry that she had spanked him.

He thought that he hadn't been away from home long enough. Perhaps Maman would still be mad at him for digging a hole with her wooden spoon. But he obediently climbed into the cart behind the brown mill horse. Pepère had bought his horse from Jacques Blanchet across the channel so he called her "the Blanchet." What else would one call a stubborn horse he had bought from a stubborn man like Jacques Blanchet?

They drove along the winding road that circled the island. It cut between farms divided among so many generations of sons that they looked like long ribbons. On the island, people lived in the old-fashioned way. It was as if time had forgotten them and they had forgotten time.

As they passed the lane that led to his home Jean-Claude looked toward the old stone house with its dormer windows and saucy turned-up brim of a roof. He could see Maman hanging up the wash, but he was sure that she was not singing at her work. He was sure that she was still angry because he had broken her spoon digging the hole.

"I will help you with the grinding, Pepère," offered Jean-Claude.

"There is not enough wind to fill a cap today," said Pepère, "but I must hoist the grain up through the trap door to the upper story so it will be ready for the hopper. You can help me with the sacks."

Jean-Claude was disappointed. Perhaps Maman was no longer angry. If only he had not dug his hole in the middle of the path.

The cart creaked slowly up Pepère's lane to his weather-beaten house covered with tar shingles. Beyond it was the squat stone mill with its pointed Pierrot cap and long skinny arms.

Memère was sitting in her rocking chair on the porch. Her face was scribbled with wrinkles and her hair looked as if it were powdered with flour like Pepère's jacket, but she had a good ear and a good foot.

"I have a touch of spring, so I came outside to see the world go by," she greeted them.

Pepère pulled La Blanchet to a stop and puffed at his pipe.

"The wild geese have arrived, Memère," cried Jean-Claude excitedly, "and we saw them come. There were millions of them, I think. And they came all at once."

"Ah, yes," said Memère. "On the Ile de Ré, the marshes were full of wild ducks and shy snipe." She pointed to the houses clustered around the church spire in the distance. "Like my village of Sainte Marie," she declared. "I can tell you that everything on your island makes me home-sick for my own. There is a great likeness between them, although mine is flat as a cake and yours puffs up on one side like a poorly beaten omelet."

Pepère pulled his shapeless hat brim lower over his fore-head. "Perhaps your island is no longer there, Annik," he said. "Perhaps it sank beneath the waves after you left."

"Such nonsense!" snapped Memère, but her eyes twinkled behind her spectacles.

Pepère was enjoying his joke. He gently jabbed the boy with his elbow. "How do we know there is an Ile de Ré any longer, my little goodman?" he asked. "Your grandmother has not heard from there in many years—not since her great-niece married."

"Tatata!" scoffed Memère. "On the Ile de Ré, we do not waste money on paper and stamps. When there is a need for it, my sister Marianne will write."

"You belong to us now, Memère," Jean-Claude reminded her. "We are your family." He hopped down from the cart. "And I am going to help Pepère with the grain sacks."

"Oh, no, you are not," said Memère. "You must march home right away. Your maman was over here looking for you."

Jean-Claude was anxious. "What did she say?" he asked.

"She said it was a nice day and that we will probably have a good summer," his grandmother replied. "She said that your brother Michel can usually be trusted and that your sister Gabie is a perfect little maman at running a house and looking after a baby."

"Did she say anything about me?" asked Jean-Claude.

"Yes, she did," Memère assured him.

"What?" asked the boy.

"Oh, this and that and such things," she replied. "I think you had better hurry home and help her hang up the wash. It is going to rain. My hens are hiding themselves. That is a sure sign of rain."

"Zut!" scoffed Pepère. "It is going to continue good for the rest of the day. There may be a few clouds, but they are leaving the north and drifting toward the east. That is a sign of clear weather."

"My hens know more about the weather than your clouds," retorted Memère. "We are going to get bad weather."

"Your hens are not sailors or they would know their weather signs better," said Pepère.

"If that is true," asked Memère, "why do they put roosters on weather vanes? In my village of Sainte Marie on Ré, the church has a rooster on its cross to tell the weather."

"Ha! But do you see a rooster on a ship's mast?" asked Pepère. "We sailors know our weather without roosters to tell us."

He clucked at La Blanchet and she needed no more urging to head for the barn.

Jean-Claude carried his nightshirt out and folded it back into his wagon.

"Do not leave until I cut you a slice of bread," said Memère. "You must be hungry after that ride to the flats."

She rose from her rocking chair and went into the house. The boy followed her into the kitchen. He watched her take a loaf of bread out of the box. She reached for the long knife and piously made the sign of the cross against the loaf with its point. Then she cut a thick slice. She buttered it generously, then sprinkled it even more generously with maple sugar from the jar.

"And do not waste a crumb," she ordered. "Bread is holy."

Jean-Claude had no intention of wasting a crumb of bread or a grain of sugar. He picked up the handle of the wagon with his free hand.

"Listen, Jean-Claude," added his grandmother, "tell your maman that you are sorry she stumbled into the hole you dug when she was carrying out the washing. Her leg might have been broken instead of the spoon. And she had to do much of the wash all over again. You have only one maman and you will never have another one."

Jean-Claude waved his slice of bread to her as he started down the lane. He was truly sorry that Maman and her clothes basket had fallen into the dirt. He hoped that Maman was sorry that she had spanked him, too.

And as he walked along, munching his bread, he could see that dark clouds were bunching over the St. Lawrence and a sudden damp breeze fanned his face.

CHAPTER TWO

It looked as if Goodman Winter had made his last farewell. Sometimes he hid away for only a week or so, then jumped out in the middle of spring with a frosty "boo." But the ice floes were gone from the river and the black wind no longer howled along the coasts.

Spring brought new plans into the younger Plouffe home. How many sacks of potatoes should be planted this year? Those from the island were said to be the best in Canada. Wouldn't it be nice to grow asters and marigolds between the rows of vegetables in the kitchen garden? There would be flowers with no waste of space. The tobacco patch was a saving too. Pepère loved his pipe in the same way that Memère loved her rocking chair.

One day Papa Plouffe took a crumpled circular from behind the clock and looked at it longingly. It advertised a wonderful tractor that would make farming easier and faster.

When Pepère came over to borrow a length of rope to mend his windmill brake, Papa showed him the advertisement as if the older man had never seen it before.

"Many of the farmers are buying these tractors now," Papa told his father. "With a machine like this, one does not need a horse. I must feed Jeanette every day whether she is working or not. But this tractor does the work of thirty horses—read it yourself, thirty horsepower—and it only eats gasoline when it works."

Pepère looked at the circular as if he had never seen it before either. Then he snorted. "*Zut!* These gasoline machines! So you buy one and for a few days it works like thirty horses. Then all of a sudden when you are in the middle of a field plowing—*crac, boum, paf!* It does not work like even one horse anymore. If you do not believe me, you have only to look in any garage on the mainland, and what do you see? Men working on these machines that have gone *crac, boum, paf*. Do you want to spend the savings for which you have worked so hard on a *crac, boum, paf* gasoline machine?"

"But I should modernize the farm," insisted Papa. "If I don't use better methods, I will never get ahead. I will only be dragging the devil by the tail all my life."

"We want to be successful," put in Maman, nervously wiping her hands on her red-checked apron.

"Successful!" snorted Pepère. "You have a strong roof over your head, plenty of food, and four fine children to honor you. What greater success is there?"

Papa hung his head like a little boy who has asked his father for something foolish.

Then the old man handed the circular back to his son. "There are new machines for grinding flour," he added, "but they do not do the job so well. Old ways are proven ways." He got up and put on his flour-sprinkled jacket. "Come, my little goodman," he said to Jean-Claude. "Come and see what an old-fashioned wind machine can do when it is mended with a little rope."

Jean-Claude followed his grandfather back to the mill. Pepère walked with slow, jerky steps as if his bones were made of wood held together by bits of rope and wire like the mill machinery.

"The wind has changed since I set the arms," noticed

Pepère. "You may hitch La Blanchet and bring her to the tail pole while I mend the brake."

The boy went into the field for the horse. La Blanchet didn't want to turn the mill pole although it was a short job—only a few steps. Jean-Claude had to force the bit into her sulky mouth, then he had to yank with all his might to get her out of the field. She rolled her eyes around wildly and tried to pull away.

"If you don't come," threatened Jean-Claude, "Pepère will buy a tractor to take your place. Then what will happen to you?"

By the time he had coaxed her to the shed and had fastened the collar around her neck, his grandfather had finished mending the brake. He came walking out of the mill door.

The tail pole reached from the Pierrot cap of the mill to the ground. Pepère hooked La Blanchet's harness to it, then started her on the circle. As the tail pole moved, it pulled the cap around and the long arms with it. Before the horse had walked a quarter of the round, the arms turned into the fickle wind again. The horse was unhooked and led back to the shed. Pepère tied her to the hitching post.

"We will keep her ready," he said. "The wind might change again."

Pepère and Jean-Claude went into the roundhouse of the mill. Pepère's white tomcat ran to the boy and rubbed its snowy sides against his legs, purring companionably. The old man looked into the bin which was half filled with flour from the chute.

Then he led Jean-Claude up the steep stairs to the upper story. This was the part of the mill that the boy loved. Here were the millstones and all the wheels and cogs. He could tilt his curly head and look way up into the cap.

Pepère pulled off the brake. Jean-Claude ran to the deep window. He climbed into it. The long arms began to turn. He could see them go by—one, two, three, four. Then they went faster and faster. Soon he could not keep up counting them because they went by so fast that he felt dizzy.

The great main shaft was turning. Everything in the mill turned with it—all the big and little wooden wheels, the cogs and shafts. Some of their parts had broken too, but Pepère had mended them with pieces of rope and wire. So everything turned as it should. The great millstones,

hidden in their frames, were roaring. Dust flew through the air, white dust and brown dust.

Jean-Claude loved the dust and the noise. He couldn't

understand why his grandmother never wanted to come into the mill when it was grinding. He wondered about the tractor and what was inside it to make the wheels go around.

He began to have a little mischievous fun with his grandfather as the old man sat at the millstones with the brake rope in hand.

"I hope Papa buys the tractor," the boy shouted into the roar of the mill. He shouted it very loudly and bravely because he knew that Pepère could not hear him above the din.

Pepère looked up and saw Jean-Claude's lips moving. He smiled and nodded.

"When Papa buys the tractor, I am going to run it," shouted Jean-Claude. "I am going—" But he shut his mouth quickly because Pepère was pulling on the brake and the rumbling slowly stopped.

"What are you saying, little man?" asked Pepère.

The boy grinned sheepishly. "I said that I can see all of Quebec from here," said Jean-Claude. He could look far across the channel to the blue Laurentian Mountains. He could see houses like blocks neatly arranged on the hilltop. He could see the boats sailing up the St. Lawrence—

trim white ships of the river fleet, lazy tramp freighters loaded with lumber from the Saguenay, and pert fishing boats.

From time to time Pepère would go down the steps to the chute below to test the flour with his thumb. Jean-Claude went with him and tried his own thumb at it.

"What do you think of the grind, my little goodman?" asked the miller.

Jean-Claude frowned as he rubbed a pinch of flour between his thumb and finger. "It is too coarse," he said. "You will have to put the stones closer together, Pepère."

Pepère clapped the boy on the back, leaving streaks of flour across his shoulders. "Ah, you have a well-made head, my little one," he said. "When I am gone, you shall have my mill."

"But, Pepère," said Jean-Claude too quickly. "I don't want to run a mill when I am a big man. I want to be a new-style farmer and drive a red tractor."

He immediately wished he had kept his mouth shut because he could tell that he had hurt his grandfather's feelings. He was glad to see the door open and Memère enter. She immediately put her hands over her ears.

"It is time for your supper, Jean-Claude," she shouted

above the mill's rumble. "The light is on in your kitchen."

Jean-Claude was surprised that it was so late. He reluctantly followed his grandmother out of the door. Why did pleasant times like grinding in a windmill go by so fast? Why did school last so long? Did time vary like the wind? Did the earth go around with the speed of a tempest sometimes and at others slow itself to a faint breeze? He wished that his head were made well enough to know all the answers.

As he walked down the lane, he looked back. The arms of the mill were turning briskly. La Blanchet was sulking in her harness and slumping on one hind leg as if the time had not passed very fast for her.

Then Jean-Claude suddenly realized that he was hungry. He was very, very hungry. He ran toward the light in the kitchen window.

He barely had time to wash his hands in the tin basin before all of the Plouffes were at the table. He bowed his head for his father's blessing of the food. But he peeped out of the corners of his eyes at his family. Papa's black mustache was hidden behind the fingers he had pressed together like a little church steeple. Michel's dark head was bowed low with earnestness. And Maman and Gabie, blonde as maple syrup, were poised lightly as if waiting to rush to the stove or cupboard for something that might have been forgotten.

As they began passing plates Jean-Claude thought about the tractor. He turned to his father.

"Why don't you buy the tractor, Papa?" he asked. "Why do you have to listen to Pepère?"

Papa settled himself more solidly into his chair and took a long, hissing swallow of the steaming pea soup.

"Jean-Claude," he said, wiping his mouth, "it is always well to ask the advice of one's father. If you had asked me about riding on the back of the old sow yesterday, I would have warned you that pigs are not to ride like horses. But you did not ask for my advice, so you were thrown into the mud and bitten by the sow."

Jean-Claude admitted this was true. "But, Papa," he still persisted, "you are a big man. Why can't you do what you want?"

Papa took another swallow of his soup. Then he shook his spoon in front of the boy's nose.

"Even a big man cannot always do as he pleases, my little one," he said. "That is, he can do it but it may hurt others. Your Pepère is an old man and already he feels left behind by the new ways. How much longer will people go on bringing their grain to his mill and baking their own bread? No, my son, I would not hurt my father's feelings by making him feel that his advice is no longer heeded by his own son."

Jean-Claude began to understand. "I know what you mean, Papa," he said. "It is like a thing Memère once told me. You have only one papa and you will never have another one. So you should keep him happy."

"That is it exactly," said Papa. "I will not go against my father's wishes." He carefully mopped the bottom of his soup plate with a piece of bread. "But I will keep talking to him about the tractor until he gets tired of listening and gives in to me."

CHAPTER THREE

It was such a clear, bright Saturday morning that the ripples of the river looked as if they were sprinkled with diamonds. Papa had hitched Jeanette to the cart. Maman, Gabie and the baby had gone with him to the village for the weekly shopping.

Then two of Michel's friends had come by in a cart pulled by a team of red and white oxen. They were going fishing for carp and wanted Michel to go with them.

Only Jean-Claude was left at home to tend the stove so it would not go out, and to scour the outdoor kettle which he had neglected to do the day before.

The boy was lonely after he finished with the kettle.

Even the stable was empty because, of course, Jeanette had gone to town too. Perhaps he would go over to his grandmother and help her. It was always fun to help Memère because she thanked and praised him for it. Maman never did that because she felt that helping around the house was a child's duty. Why should one be praised and thanked for doing his duty? Did anyone thank her for doing the cooking, the washing and all the other housework?

Jean-Claude lifted the stove lid and pushed some more wood through the hole. Yes, he would go to visit his grandmother.

Memère was in the fowl yard scattering grain husks to the red chickens. She wore her "kiss not" as she called the wide-brimmed sunbonnet like those worn by the women on the Ile de Ré.

"Jean-Claude, my little one," she greeted him. "How nice of you to come over to visit me. I am all alone with nothing for company but my rocking chair."

"I will feed the chickens for you," offered Jean-Claude.

He took the bowl from her hand and flung the husks this way and that. He liked to fool the chickens by pretending that he was going to throw their food in one direc-

tion, and then tossing it in the other. He laughed at the way the foolish chickens bumped into each other and squawked as they ran for the husks.

"What a helpful little man you are!" exclaimed Memère. "Your parents are very lucky to have such a helpful son."

Jean-Claude let the curly bang hide his eyes. "They have all gone away," he said. "And they left me alone."

"Come into the house and I will find some cakes for you," said Memère.

She stopped at the porch steps to look over the island and the sparkling river from under the great brim of her "kiss not."

"Ah, the air is so clear today that the light brings everything closer," she said. "It is like this on my Ile de Ré. That is why it is called the Island of Light."

"Tell me more about your island, Memère," urged Jean-Claude. "Are there oxen and horses and pigs and chickens there?"

"Of course," she replied, "but also something there which we do not have here on your island. There are donkeys that wear trousers."

"Donkeys in trousers?" repeated the boy, as if he had never heard of them before from Memère's lips.

"Yes," answered Memère, and really she could not remember if she had ever told Jean-Claude about the donkeys in trousers before. "A pair of blue-checked calico trousers on their front legs and sometimes on their hind ones also," said Memère. "Fashioned to the cut of the donkey."

"Why do they wear trousers?" asked the boy.

Memère was sure that he had asked that question before and that she had answered it. "Why do you think?" she returned *tac* for *tac*.

Jean-Claude smiled. "So they will look elegant?" he asked.

"No," said his grandmother, reaching into the crock.

"To keep them warm?" asked the boy, holding out his hand for a cake.

"No," answered Memère. "Do the horses and oxen on this island need trousers to keep them warm? And I can tell you that it gets much colder here than there."

"Then why do the donkeys on the Ile de Ré wear trousers, Memère?" asked Jean-Claude although his mouth was full of cake. Before she could speak, he quickly answered himself. "So they won't be bitten by the flies and mosquitoes on your island."

"That is right, Jean-Claude," said Memère, "but you

must not talk with your mouth full of cake." Then Memère said something which she had never said to him before. "Can you imagine La Blanchet in trousers?" she grinned. "It would be a droll sight."

Jean-Claude's half smile turned into a bubbling laugh.

It was almost impossible to imagine La Blanchet walking the mill round with trousers on her legs. But the more Jean-Claude thought about it, the clearer he could see the picture.

All the way home to put more wood on the fire, he imagined La Blanchet in trousers. When he went into the woodshed, he saw Papa's blue work trousers hanging on a nail. He imagined the horse in them. He laughed some more.

He would put Papa's trousers on the mill horse. Watch the surprised look on Memère's face when he would lead La Blanchet up to the porch to show her.

Jean-Claude rolled the trousers into a ball and went back to his grandparents' place. He ran quickly past the door so that Memère would not see him. He wanted to surprise her.

La Blanchet was grazing in the field when Jean-Claude climbed the rail fence. She raised her head and looked at him questioningly. If he was carrying a bridle, she would bolt. But what he was carrying had no likeness to a bridle. She put her head down and began chomping the weeds again.

Jean-Claude went to her hindquarters and studied them carefully. Since he had only one pair of trousers, he decided that was the proper place for them. How would he ever get the trousers on her? It was hard enough to get a bit into her mouth. And her knees were in back of her legs instead of in front like Papa's. She would have to wear Papa's trousers backwards.

Then he remembered how the blacksmith lifted her hoofs, one at a time, between his knees when he shod her. La Blanchet never minded that.

Jean-Claude began pulling at her leg with all his might. "Up, up," he shouted, as he had heard the blacksmith do.

La Blanchet lazily raised her hoof and Jean-Claude pulled one trouser a little way up her leg. Then he went to her other side. "Up, up, La Blanchet," he ordered. "You are going to be very chic—like the donkeys on Memère's island."

About this time, the horse became suspicious. She realized that she wasn't being shod and she wasn't being harnessed. Something unusual and frightening was being done to her.

She let out a shrill "*henisse, henisse.*" She kicked her legs into the air. If Jean-Claude hadn't raised himself to pull the top of the trousers under her tail, she would have kicked his head off. As it was, he was thrown to the ground.

Cri-i-ic went Papa's trousers as the horse galloped to the end of the pasture. They had ripped in two. One trouser was lying on the grass and the other had twisted around

La Blanchet's hoof as she stopped at the far fence.

Hélas! What would Papa say when he saw his trousers in two pieces?

Jean-Claude picked up the trouser leg near him, then went after the horse to get the other. But La Blanchet no longer trusted him. She whinnied again and galloped away. Around the pasture he chased her. By the time Papa's other trouser leg came loose from her hoof, it was torn into three pieces.

Jean-Claude's heart was heavy. He gathered the trouser legs into his arms and went to look for Memère. He found her in the kitchen.

"What are you doing with those old rags?" she asked.

The boy's eyes filled with tears, but he brushed them away with a piece of trouser. "They aren't rags, Memère," he said. "They are Papa's work trousers."

"Wherever did your father wear them that they are in such a state?" asked Memère.

"It wasn't Papa who wore them," said Jean-Claude. "It was La Blanchet. Can you please mend them, Memère, so Papa won't know that a horse wore them?"

In tumbling words he told his grandmother how he had put the trousers on the mill horse.

"Jean-Claude," cried his grandmother, "that was very wicked. Where did you get such a crazy idea?"

"From you, Memère," sniffled the boy. "It was your idea."

"How can you say such a thing!" exclaimed Memère. "I would never have such an idea."

"Oh, yes, you did," accused Jean-Claude. "You said for me to imagine La Blanchet wearing trousers like the donkeys on your island. And I did. So I tried to put the trousers on her."

"Now, now, Jean-Claude Plouffe," she cried. "You are not going to lay the blame for your folly on your poor old grandmother. I did not tell you to do it."

"But you put the idea in my head," insisted Jean-Claude. "Pepère says I have a well-made head, but I never would have thought of such a thing by myself."

Memère was in a huff, but she searched through her sewing basket for needle and thread. She sat down in her rocking chair and sewed the two legs and the pieces of trousers together as carefully and neatly as if she were making a coverlet from knit squares.

She handed them back to the boy in one piece. "Listen, little one," she said. "Take them home and confess to your

Papa what you have done. Never try to hide misdeeds because they are sure to stick out somewhere."

Jean-Claude took the trousers back. He hoped that his parents hadn't returned from the village yet. He hoped they would stay away until dark. He hoped they might even spend the night with Maman's cousin who lived near the church.

Michel had just come back with a string of carp. "What have you got there?" he asked Jean-Claude curiously.

"Something Memère sewed for Papa," answered the younger boy truthfully.

Oh, là, the rest of the family were home too. They hadn't stayed in the village until dark, and even Jeanette knew they wouldn't have spent the night there.

"Hello, my little man," Papa greeted him. "Have you been a good boy while we were gone?"

"No, Papa," answered Jean-Claude bravely. "I have been very wicked."

He held up the trousers.

"Where did you find those old things?" asked Papa. "In the ditch? I surely don't want such old patched trousers when I have my good ones."

"These are your good trousers," answered the boy. "La

Blanchet was wearing them. Can you imagine trousers on a horse, Papa?"

Papa could not imagine his trousers on La Blanchet, so the boy had to explain it twice.

"Name of a blue donkey!" roared his father when he finally was able to imagine such a sight. "Where did you ever get such a crazy idea?"

The boy cast his eyes down. He didn't want to tell on Memère. He felt that he should protect her from Papa's anger. She had done so much for him.

"I got the crazy idea all by myself," said Jean-Claude. He felt very noble for taking the blame.

"A boy who does such a thing deserves a good whipping," said Papa sternly. "Go to the woodpile and pick out the right kind of a stick. Not heavy enough to break a bone. Not too brittle that it will snap after a couple of blows. Just the right size to teach a small boy that he must not put his father's trousers on a horse."

"Yes, Papa," said Jean-Claude.

He went to the woodpile. He picked up a stick of wood. It was too big, that one. It would make Papa's arm very tired. He picked up another. The bark was peeling from it. It might bruise Papa's hand. He picked up a long, tough twig and reaching behind, gave himself a little switch. *Ouche!* That one was just right.

Jean-Claude took the twig back to his father. Papa looked into the boy's sad brown eyes. He looked at the tear smudges on his cheeks. Then he looked at the long, tough twig.

"A very good choice," said his father. "Now take it into the house and put it in the woodbox. It will be useful for starting a fire. And, Jean-Claude, if you ever take my trousers off the nail again, I will give you such a whipping that you will not be able to wear your own for a week."

CHAPTER FOUR

When the frogs begin to cry "quick, quick," it is time to do the spring planting in French Canada. On the river banks, a chorus of frogs kept warning the farmers.

Papa Plouffe heeded their piping voices and quickly finished plowing his potato field. Already the old potatoes had been cut into pieces which would start new plants.

Jean-Claude liked to help his father plant the pieces of potato in the long furrows when he had a school holiday.

"Be sure to turn each eye up," ordered his father, "and space them so far apart." He spread his feet apart to show how far the pieces should be separated.

Jean-Claude worked carefully if not as quickly as the frogs might have wished. His eyes measured the distance between his feet, and his hands set the pieces of potato, eyes up.

Then he straightened and asked, "Papa, why do we sometimes call potatoes 'apples of the earth'?"

"Because they are under the ground," answered Papa impatiently. He didn't want to waste time in talk.

"Then why aren't the apples you store in the cave 'apples of the earth' since they are under the ground?" asked the boy.

"Don't talk so much or you won't be able to keep up with me," ordered his father.

Jean-Claude leaned over again, but his head was as busy as his hands and feet.

"If we cut apples into pieces and planted them like this, would they grow potato plants?" the boy soon asked.

Papa was annoyed. "Little man," he said, "an apple tree grows from an apple seed and a potato plant from the eye of a potato."

"Why?" persisted the boy.

Papa frowned and stamped at the furrow. "Jean-Claude," he cried, "you are like a little black fly in my ear. Michel is in the wagon shed. Go and see if you can help him with whatever he is doing."

Jean-Claude tossed his sack of cut potatoes on the ground. As he stumbled over the furrows he began to smile his half smile. Wouldn't it be funny if Maman brought some apples from the cave to make tarts and they turned into potato tarts?

In the shed Michel was cleaning the cage in which he kept his pet porcupine. Picpic had come down the Saguenay River on a barge of logs. A sailor had discovered the stowaway and had given him to Michel at the ferry dock one day. The children on the island had dogs and cats and even lambs and piglets for pets, but no one save Michel had a porcupine.

The older boy had let Picpic loose in the shed while he cleaned his cage. The porcupine was chewing on an ax handle.

"Stop that, Picpic," cried Michel, pulling the ax away from the porcupine's yellow teeth. "You must not eat Papa's ax handle."

"Perhaps he is trying to help," said Jean-Claude. "Like I was trying to help Papa."

Michel laughed and stooped over the porcupine. He petted its head and back. Jean-Claude put his hand down to pet the porcupine too.

"No, no," warned his brother. "You will get your hand full of quills."

"But you are petting him, Mich'," protested the younger boy.

"I know *how*," replied Michel in a very big-brother tone of voice. "You must never pet a porcupine unless you know how to do it."

"Will you show me?" asked Jean-Claude.

"I'm too busy," said Michel. "Can't you see I'm cleaning his cage? Then I have to oil the harnesses."

Jean-Claude slipped his hands into the pockets of the overalls that had belonged to Michel first. He watched his brother finish sweeping the cage. He watched him coax the porcupine back into it and fasten the door.

"And don't try to pet him," repeated Michel, "or you'll

get stuck with quills. Then you'll bawl like a calf and Papa will make me get rid of Picpic."

Michel went to the harness room. Jean-Claude stood with his hands in his pockets watching the porcupine.

Picpic grunted and shook his quills. Then he clumsily rose to his hind legs. He stamped from one foot to the other with his shoulders hunched and his glizzled head swaying from side to side—like Titi Dufour at the square dances.

Jean-Claude looked around. Michel wasn't in sight. He quickly loosed the cage door. How could he learn to pet a porcupine if he didn't try? He reached in gingerly. He fingered a tuft of the long black hairs that guarded the sharp quills.

Picpic was taken by surprise. He raised his quills in warning. He slapped his tail against the side of the cage. A few quills loosened from it and two of them struck the boy's outstretched hand. *Ouche!*

Jean-Claude smothered a cry lest Michel should hear him. He dropped to his knees with a little whimper. He mustn't cry out loud. He tugged one quill out and then the other. *Ouche! Ouche!* His mouth was turned upside down and a tear rolled out of each eye, but he didn't make a sound.

He looked at the long quills with their sharp points. They looked like giant needles. What would Memère say if she knew that he had been stuck by such needles but had not cried? He proudly pinned the quills onto his shirt. He would give them to Memère when he saw her again.

"Jean-Claude!" His brother's voice coming from behind made him jump. "You have let Picpic out of his cage," cried his brother, "when I especially told you to let him alone."

It was that way. The pain of the quills had made the younger boy forget all about the open door of the cage. Picpic had shuffled out and was busy gnawing on the handle of the scythe.

"I wanted to learn to pet Picpic," said Jean-Claude stubbornly.

"You are a naughty little goblin," scolded his brother. "If you try to pet him, you'll get stuck with quills. Don't you believe me?"

Jean-Claude put his right hand back in his pocket and solemnly nodded. "Yes, Mich'," he agreed. "I believe you."

"Then leave him alone or you'll be sorry," said Michel. "Why don't you carry some wood into the house for Gabie? She is minding Bébé and the soup while Maman puts away the winter woolens."

Jean-Claude turned his back on Michel and his pet porcupine. He went to the woodpile and carefully looked over the logs to see that no porcupine had come in on the load from the woods. He picked up two sticks and carried them into the kitchen.

Gabie was rocking the baby in the wooden cradle that had nursed so many generations of Plouffes.

Jean-Claude threw the sticks into the woodbox, then ran to the cradle.

"Chut!" warned his sister in a loud whisper. "Bébé is asleep."

Jean-Claude stared down at the little face that looked so much like that of the angels in the painting at church.

"May I play with her?" he asked.

"C-chut!" whispered Gabie again. "Of course you can't play with her when she is sleeping. But you may rock the cradle while I go make the beds now that they've been aired. Easy, now. Don't awaken her."

Jean-Claude began to rock the cradle. He rocked it gently as a canoe on the water. The baby smiled in her sleep and the boy knew that was a sign that she was talking to the angels. He rocked her faster and faster so that she would sleep more soundly and have a longer visit with the angels. He rocked her so hard that she was tossed from side to side. She opened her eyes and began to cry.

The boy quickly lifted her into his arms to quiet her. He rocked her back and forth in them, looking tenderly

into the clear blue eyes that Maman said might turn brown like his own. She was soft and warm. She was much nicer than an old porcupine full of stickers.

Then his sister returned to the kitchen. "Jean-Claude," she gasped, "how dare you take up the baby when I distinctly told you not to? You are always into things—like a cow's tail."

Jean-Claude thrust his chin out and went up the steps to sulk in the bedroom he shared with Michel.

Maman was upstairs arranging the woolens to store in the big wooden chest that was a hundred years old. Jean-Claude recognized his long red stocking cap. He yanked it out of the pile and pulled it over his curly hair. He thought of the good times he had worn it skating on the ice and sledding down the hills. There at the bottom was the heavy scarf that matched. He pulled at the scarf and the whole pile fell over.

"Jean-Claude," cried Maman, "you are mixing up all the woolens I have sorted so carefully. Why don't you be a useful little boy and go help your father plant the potatoes?"

Jean-Claude went to his bed and pulled his nightshirt

from under his pillow. "I am going to live with Memère," he said. "Everyone is mad at me."

"That is a good idea," said Maman, "but be back in time to drive the cow home."

The boy went to the kitchen, carrying his nightshirt. "I am going to live with Memère and Pepère," he told Gabie, in case she hadn't noticed what he was carrying.

"I wish you would," retorted his sister angrily, because Bébé was still crying even though Gabie was rocking her cradle.

When Jean-Claude arrived at his grandparents' house, he met Memère bringing in the eggs. She looked at his nightshirt in the wagon.

"Hé! Hô!" she exclaimed. "So what have you done now? Did you put your maman's cap on Jeanette's ears or did you put Jeanette's harness on the cow. Or did—." But she quickly tightened her lips because she did not want to put such ideas into Jean-Claude's well-made head.

"No," grumbled the boy. "I only tried to help them and they got mad at me. I don't think they want me in their family."

"How could you get such an idea?" scoffed Memère.

"Because they don't like me," said the boy. "I am in the wrong family."

Memère set the basket of eggs down on the porch. She twisted her strong, crooked fingers around the boy's shoulders.

"Listen, Jean-Claude," she said. "We make our friends ourselves, but the good God gives us our families. He chooses just the right people to put together for a family—although sometimes we may find that hard to believe." Jean-Claude imagined the good God in heaven carving little wooden figures like Odilon Dufour with his knife and gouge. He imagined Him arranging them into groups to make the different families. "So members of a family should live together in love and peace," finished Memère.

"They don't want me to live with them," quavered Jean-Claude, feeling more and more sorry for himself. He began thinking that his hand still hurt from the quill pricks. "Even the porcupine doesn't like me," he began to sob.

He showed her the two red spots on his hand. "Picpic threw his quills at me," he wept.

"Then stay away from him," said Memère sensibly.

"Come and let me rub a little chicken fat on the *bobos,* and they will heal quickly."

After she had rubbed his sores with chicken fat, the boy proudly showed her the quills which had made them. "They are for you, Memère," he said. "Perhaps Pepère will make holes in them, then you will have two big needles."

His grandmother exclaimed at the size of the quills. She brought out her plump pincushion and Jean-Claude proudly stuck them among the glass-headed pins. He thought that the pincushion looked like a little porcupine.

"I have just baked some apple tarts," said Memère, "and I am going to give you one so you will get some sense into your head. A well-filled stomach makes for straight thoughts. Then you must go back to your family and give them another chance."

Jean-Claude ate the juicy tart. He was glad that it wasn't made from apples of the earth.

"Maybe they won't let me come back," he said, because he hadn't finished feeling sorry for himself and he was hungry for another tart. "Perhaps they will slam the door at my nose."

"*Tatata!*" exclaimed Memère. "Have they ever slammed the door at your nose when you've returned home? You are not thinking straight yet. Here, have another tart."

After Jean-Claude had eaten his second tart, he began thinking a straight thought. He began thinking that if he didn't get to the pasture and drive the cow home, he would be in more trouble with his family.

So he pulled his wagon away. As he walked along, he thought that probably the good God had put the Plouffe family together properly except that He hadn't carved Jean-Claude in the right size. If he were bigger than Gabie and Michel, they couldn't boss him. If he were tiny like Bébé, he would receive all of the attention and no punishment.

He took his wagon to the shed first. Michel had finished oiling the harnesses. He seemed to have forgotten that he had scolded his brother.

"I'm going to take Picpic out and give him some cabbage leaves," he said, "so I'll have time to show you how to pet him."

Jean-Claude squirmed. "I don't think I want to learn to pet him," he answered. "After all, he belongs to you."

"Oh, come," said Michel. "Picpic won't hurt you."

"He might throw some quills at me," said Jean-Claude. "He might throw two of them into my hand."

"He wouldn't do that," promised Michel. "A porcupine can't really throw his quills. But you have to pet him the right way if you don't want to get stuck. Come, I'll show you."

"I don't want to pet him, Mich'," insisted Jean-Claude. "I'd rather watch you."

"Then you can feed him a cabbage leaf," said Michel agreeably.

So the older boy petted Picpic while Jean-Claude fed the porcupine a wilted cabbage leaf with his left hand so Michel wouldn't see the pricks on his right one.

Then the little boy took his nightshirt out of the wagon and headed for the house.

"I was looking for you, Jean-Claude," said Gabie. "Bébé is awake now and you can hold her if you want."

Jean-Claude was really out of the mood for holding Bébé, but he knew that Gabie was trying to show that she was sorry for the things she had said to him. So he sat in the rocking chair and stiffly held Bébé. He rocked her back and forth, back and forth, in the hope that she would fall asleep again and he would be freed.

Then Maman came down the stairs. "Why, Jean-Claude," she said, "what a helpful little boy you are—

taking care of your baby sister. I don't know what we would do without you. I will take her so you can go after the cow."

As he went past the barn toward the pasture Jean-Claude met his father coming home from the potato field. Papa had made him a flute from an alder branch. There were six holes of different sizes cut in the flute so that if the fingers were worked over them, Jean-Claude could blow a tune.

He walked up the cowpath trying to play "Alouette" on

his alder flute. He would play music for the cow all the way back to the barn. He blew louder and louder into the flute, turning all of his happiness into gay notes. *Tou-ite! Tou-ite!* He began to dance down the path to his music.

He was sure now that he was in the right family. God had chosen His best carvings for Plouffes. *Oui,* the good God knew the kind of people who belonged together.

CHAPTER FIVE

It was Danielle Boulet who brought the terrifying letter to the Plouffe home. She came racing down the road with her bare feet scattering the pebbles. Behind her ran the little Boulet dog harnessed to the tiny wagon which Danielle had trained him to pull like a big work dog.

Jean-Claude jumped down from his perch on the rail fence and hurried to Danielle. He knew that she had come from the village, and he hoped that she brought some excitement. It was vacation time and he had a dull morning trying to amuse himself. Of course, Papa could have used some help in weeding the garden, but Jean-Claude did not think that pulling weeds was amusing.

Danielle scarcely stopped to greet him, and the dog went on with the wagon.

"A letter from France for your grandmother," cried Danielle. "Maman said I must bring it to your parents first."

"I'll take it to them," offered the boy.

"No," refused Danielle, "it is too important for you. *I* must give the letter with my own hand. That is what Maman told me."

She began running again and Jean-Claude followed behind her, disgusted that a freckle-faced, spindly little girl like Danielle Boulet was thought more trustworthy for delivering a letter.

"What's in it?" panted Jean-Claude.

"Do I open my neighbor's letters?" called Danielle over her shoulder. "The envelope is thin but I couldn't read through it."

The children, the dog and the cart raced up the Plouffe lane. Maman came from the vegetable cave carrying a basket of old potatoes.

"A letter for Memère," shouted Jean-Claude, with what he thought was his last breath because he had run so fast. But he felt it was his right to break the news even if he couldn't be trusted to carry the letter.

Maman dropped the basket and some of the potatoes rolled over the ground. She seized the letter and stared at it with frightened eyes. She held it up to the light, hoping she might be able to read a few words through the thin envelope.

Danielle loitered with the dog. "I brought it all the way from the post office because Maman had to stay in the village," she said, hoping for the reward of a piece of cake or a slice of pie.

Maman hardly heard Danielle because her mind was on the letter in her hand.

"Thank you," she replied hastily. "Thank you very much, Danielle."

The girl's freckled face dropped. She called to the dog. Roi hung his head and his tail, and turned his wagon to follow. He had hoped for a crumb or a bone as his reward.

Jean-Claude could scarcely wait to find out what was in the letter.

"What does it say, Maman?" he asked. "Why don't you open it?"

"The letter is addressed to Memère," said Maman reprovingly. "Get your father immediately. He may feel it is his duty to open it."

Jean-Claude raced out to the potato field to find Papa stooped among the young plants.

"A letter from France," Jean-Claude cried to him as he tried to hop between the green rows. "It's for Memère."

Papa rose to his feet quickly. "What does it say?" he asked.

"I don't know," replied Jean-Claude. "Nobody knows because nobody will open it."

Papa made giant steps to the house with Jean-Claude trying to keep up with him. Michel quickly joined them.

Maman handed Papa the letter. Papa studied the stamps and the return address. "It is indeed from France," he agreed, "but it is not from my Aunt Marianne. She must be dead."

Maman burst into tears. Although she had never known Memère's sister, a notice of death was a sad event and tears were fitting. "Poor Memère!" she sobbed.

"Aren't you going to open it?" asked Jean-Claude.

"Would I open mail not addressed to me?" asked Papa with Maman's words. "But perhaps I can read through the envelope."

He pressed the thin paper against its contents but had no more success than Maman. "Of one thing we can be sure," he decided. "It is bad news. Misfortune has come to my mother. We will go as a family to console her. Where is Gabie?"

"I saw her go down the road toward the Boulets," put in Jean-Claude, proud that something worthwhile had come from sitting on the rail fence.

"She went to knit and gossip with Jeanne," said Maman.

"Go and get her," ordered Papa. "We must go as a family. The Plouffes have always shared their joys together. It is only right that now we should share Memère's grief with her."

Jean-Claude retraced his steps down the lane as fast as he had come up it with Danielle and her dog.

At the end of it, he met Memère and Pepère returning

from the ferry dock in their two-wheeled cart. He did not dare tell them about the letter. It was Papa's place to break the news.

"Where are you going in such a rush, my little good-man?" asked Pepère, drawing up on La Blanchet's reins.

"I can't tell you," Jean-Claude informed him. "And you better go right home. We're all coming to see you."

Memère looked worried. "I must have forgotten some-body's feast day," she said, "although today is St. Raoul's and no one is named after him. I must get a cake into the oven fast."

Fortunately Gabie was already on her way back because Danielle had told her about the letter when she arrived home with Roi. She raced back with Jean-Claude.

At last the whole Plouffe family was gathered on the porch.

"What shall we do with Bébé?" asked Maman. "Her bottle isn't ready yet. Shouldn't Jean-Claude stay home and give it to her?"

Jean-Claude's heart skipped a beat at the thought of missing out on the excitement, but Papa soon reassured him.

"Bébé must go too," said Papa. "We must go as a

family." He glanced at Bébé who was fretting for her bottle. "One is never too young to learn that there is death and Paradise as well as birth," he said.

So the whole Plouffe family tramped down the lane with Jean-Claude running from heel to heel and speeding them along like a sheep dog.

Memère and Pepère were standing on their own porch waiting for them because Memère already had her cake in the oven.

"I can't imagine what day we have forgotten," said Memère. "Perhaps it is only someone's birthday." In French Canada, one's birthday is never as important as that of his name saint.

"I am sure it is not mine," said Pepère. "I will not be born until next month."

At the sight of the letter, Memère sank weakly into the rocking chair.

Papa handed the letter to her. "God's will be done," he said softly. "Regardless of what bad news it contains, my mother, our sympathies are with you. You still have us alive and in good health."

Merère examined the letter that trembled in her crooked fingers. She peered through her glasses at the strange stamps and the strange name which did not belong to anyone in her family.

"Why would a stranger write to me?" she asked in a broken voice. "Why not one of the relatives on my island? Death is a family matter."

She put the letter in her lap and stared at it some more. Maman began to weep again and Gabie joined her. Then Bébé puckered her tiny face and began wailing because she wanted her bottle.

Jean-Claude thought that Pepère had the most sensible idea. "Open the letter, Annik," he demanded. "Must we itch with worry while you play with the envelope?"

But he had to open it because Memère's fingers were trembling too much. He pulled out the sheets and handed them to his wife, but her fingers shook the pages so that she could not read them. She gave the letter to Papa. She leaned back in her chair, closed her eyes and silently moved her lips in prayer.

Papa's dark eyes were pulled from their sockets by the words on the paper. His own fingers began to tremble.

"Read it out loud," demanded Pepère, but Papa did not do so. At last he deliberately folded the pages. He stretched out his hand to his mother. "Congratulations, my mother," he said. "You have inherited a sturdy two-story dwelling in the village of Sainte Marie on the Ile de Ré. Your old employer has died and willed it to you. His lawyer has written this letter."

For a few moments the room was silent as the inside of an oven. Memère's hands stopped trembling. Her eyes seemed to look through the walls.

"Ah, I remember good Monsieur Morin well," she said. "And his pretty wife who died so young. Many years I worked for them, and they always treated me like one of the family."

A slow fear closed in on Jean-Claude. "But you weren't really, Memère," he said. "We are your family."

Then Memère laughed and patted his dark head.

"You are a rich woman now, Annik," joked Pepère. "Perhaps I shall retire from my mill."

"*Tatata!*" scoffed Memère. "I am rich because I have such a fine family on this island. But I will have to go back to Ré to attend to my inheritance."

Jean-Claude felt that his fears had been justified. "You won't be gone long, will you, Memère?" he asked anxiously.

"Of course she won't be gone long," put in Pepère,

"because I am going with her. And you know well that I will be in a hurry to return."

Then there was a *herla berla* of congratulations and plans for the trip. They would sail from Quebec city. Papa would see about the tickets. Maman would help them with the packing.

"And I'll take care of the house and mill while you're gone," offered Jean-Claude.

"We'll all take care of your place," Papa assured them.

Memère's mind was not on the plans. "I remember the white house with the green shutters," she daydreamed, "and the narrow winding street with flowerpots at each doorway. And I liked to go barefoot into the marshes and gather bouquets of the little wild sea pinks. I loved their spicy smell."

"Gabie and I often gather daisies for you and they have a spicy smell too," said Jean-Claude reproachfully. He was jealous of the Ile de Ré because it was not his island.

But Memère didn't act as if she heard him. As she went on talking about her island, she seemed to grow young again. Her eyes brightened and her cheeks pinked. She was the young girl whom Pepère had met at a fête on the Ile de Ré.

Jean-Claude didn't want his memère to be that young girl. He had never known her. She was a stranger from across the sea.

"That was a long time ago, Memère," he said, "and you didn't have me then."

Memère quickly returned to her old self because a sharp smell of burning cake floated to the porch. "The cake," she cried. "The anniversary cake."

They all followed her into the kitchen and soon the blackened remains of the cake were scraped into the sink.

"It isn't even fit for the chickens," said Memère ruefully.

Pepère looked disappointed, but he comforted her. "It is right that it should burn, Annik," he said. "It was baked for someone's birthday or feast day and this is no such day."

But the burnt cake reminded Maman of something else. "I should have given Danielle a piece of our chocolate cake for going to all that trouble of bringing the letter," she said. "It is getting stale anyway."

CHAPTER SIX

All of the Plouffes went as a family to help Memère and Pepère pack for their trip to the Ile de Ré.

Memère had never owned many dresses, but she was rich in petticoats. The old suitcases loaned by a neighbor would not hold all of them. Pepère went to the mill for a clean flour sack, and that was quickly stuffed. There were still the towels Memère insisted on taking, and Pepère's packets of homegrown tobacco. Memère didn't want the tobacco packed with her towels, so Gabie ran back to their house and found a cardboard box.

"You are only going for a trip, my mother," said Papa when Memère began finding more things she wanted to take with her.

Marianne, her sister, would enjoy some loaves of maple sugar since they did not have that delicacy in France. And of course she wanted to take the framed picture of the family made on Bébé's baptismal day. And she mustn't forget her "kiss not" hanging by the door, so she would be in style back on her island.

"I have to decide so many things that I don't know which foot to dance on." Memère sighed.

Michel rode La Blanchet over to the Boulets' farm and was able to get a strong paper bag with handles.

"My umbrella," cried Memère. "We must take the umbrella because it rains a great deal on my island."

Papa obligingly lashed the umbrella to the suitcase with twine. This reminded Memère that she should take her rubbers and Pepère would need his rubber boots. "You will probably want to visit the oyster beds and the salt pools," she told him. "Everyone on my island has boots."

Papa cleverly pushed Memère's rubbers into Pepère's boots then tied the boots together, making a string handle.

"And you must be sure to use the food I will be leaving in the cupboard," Memère told Maman. "Nothing must go to waste."

"Don't worry about that," said Papa. "Don't worry about anything. We will take care of your property while you are gone."

"I'll keep your house swept and dusted," offered Gabie.

"And I'll gather the eggs and feed the chickens," said Maman.

"I'll bring La Blanchet to our barn and stable her with Jeanette," said Michel. "Don't worry about her."

"And I'll take care of the mill," promised Jean-Claude. "I'll keep the bins clean and chase the pigeons out of the cap. And I'll bring the cat home. He can sleep in our barn."

"Don't forget to gather the apples from the tree by the back porch when they are ripe," said Memère. "They are the best for jelly."

"Aren't you coming back before *then?*" asked Jean-Claude unhappily. "When are you coming back?"

"Such a boy," put in Pepère. "We have not left yet, and already he is asking when we are coming back."

"That depends on how soon I can dispose of Monsieur Morin's house," explained Memère.

Jean-Claude had an idea in his well-made head. "Why can't Great-Aunt Marianne sell your house for you?" he asked. "Why don't you write her a letter about it? I'll help you unpack all your things and put them back in place. I'll take the suitcase back to Madame Gignac and the bag to the Boulets."

Everyone laughed at Jean-Claude's idea, and half of his mouth smiled too.

"One must tend to his own business, Jean-Claude," said Memère. "When one wants a thing done right, he should do it himself."

Jean-Claude had another idea. "Why don't you take me

with you?" he asked. "Why don't we all go to see your island?"

"And who would take care of Papa's farm then?" asked Memère. "I can tell you that fruit and vegetables do not cultivate and harvest themselves. And who would feed the animals? They certainly won't do it themselves."

"Who would take care of my mill?" asked Pepère. "The rats?"

Jean-Claude could see that his idea was not well made.

But all the family got to go with Memère and Pepère on the trip to take them to the railroad station across the channel.

They went in the blue wagon with Papa driving and Maman and Memère squeezed on the seat to the left of him. They had put a chair in the wagon bed for Gabie to sit on while holding Bébé. Pepère, Michel and Jean-Claude stood up, their hands on the back of the seat.

As they drove away, La Blanchet stood at the fence corner, sadly watching the departure. Jean-Claude wondered if she thought everyone was leaving and that she would truly have to feed herself.

The wheels crunched over the road that circled the island. Everyone tried to be very gay, as if they were going on a picnic instead of driving Memère and Pepère away. Truly it looked like a picnic with all the bags and cartons, and the extra basket of food which Maman had fixed for a lunch to be eaten on the train to Quebec.

Neighbors came to their doorways to wave good-bye. Memère and Pepère smiled happily. They had received so many good wishes that their trip would surely be safe and successful.

"Ah, it will feel good to get the deck under my feet again," said Pepère, remembering his sailing days.

"Look," cried Jean-Claude as they drove down the winding hill to the dock. "There comes the ferry now."

They could see the flat boat crossing the channel. Jean-Claude was full of excitement. He would have a boat ride, anyway, even if it would be only across the St. Lawrence instead of the ocean. It wasn't often that he got to ride the ferry—only on All Saints' Day when they drove to the mainland to sweep the graves of Maman's parents and decorate them with paper flowers.

There were others waiting at the dock. There were two of the regular trucks that brought provisions to the island. Pierre LaForge and his dog were driving a herd of sheep to a farm in the mountains. Madame Gignac was on her

way to visit her daughter in Baie St. Paul with a month's gossip and a new recipe for plum preserves.

The ferry boat bumped against the dock. Men threw the mooring ropes. An unsteady plank bridge was laid from the dock to the flat deck. The passengers surged forward, all but Madame Gignac who feared being squeezed by the sheep.

Jeanette didn't want to take a boat ride. Halfway across the plank, she sensed that it wasn't solid. She snorted and began to back. Maman screamed and Papa used the whip on her. If it hadn't been for the dock workers, the cart might have upset, and then what would have happened to the bags and bundles and Plouffes?

But two workmen grabbed Jeanette by the bridle, another pulled at her collar and Papa reached his foot out and pushed against her backside. Snorting and wildly rolling her eyes, Jeanette rocked the plank as she danced across it. Jean-Claude fearfully looked down to see that the wheels were following on the makeshift bridge.

Soon they were safely on the ferry and surrounded by restless sheep. Michel and Jean-Claude jumped down from the wagon to lean against the rail so they wouldn't miss anything. The whistle blew, Jeanette snorted, the sheep began playing follow the leader around the trucks, and Madame Gignac went to the snack stand to buy a bag of potato chips to fortify her during the trip.

The small ferry slowly zigzagged across the channel, guided by the ripples and the colors of the water. Jean-Claude's eager eyes swept the river. He saw the seagulls. He saw the red and white lighthouse. He saw a tugboat pulling a raft of lumber. Then he yelled and pointed. In the distant water, white backs were breaking through the surface.

"The white whales," cried Michel. "We must be in a whole school of them."

It made Jean-Claude dizzy trying to look at all the whales turning through the water like white wheels.

The wooded shore and the blue mountains came closer and closer, as if they were moving instead of the boat. Then the long, gray dock on the mainland bumped the ferry. They had arrived.

Everyone waited for the trucks to get off. Madame Gignac swallowed her last potato chip. And when Jeanette's turn came, she bolted across the planks as if she couldn't get ashore fast enough.

It was a short drive to the railroad station. It sat beside

the tracks that followed the shore line. The Plouffes were early so they had plently of time to stack the baggage beside the tracks and explore the station. Papa restlessly studied the timetables and read the posted signs.

Memère gave her last instructions. "Now did I tell you not to forget the food left in the cupboard?" she asked anxiously. "And I don't remember if I mentioned the apples. The ones on the tree by the back porch make wonderful jelly. Don't forget to pick them."

Then they heard the train whistle, and the black engine swiftly glided toward them. Jean-Claude had enjoyed the outing so far. But now he was filled with panic. He burst into tears and clung to Memère like a little bird to its perch in a windstorm.

"*Bouhou, bouhou.* Don't go away, Memère," he wept.

His grandmother had to stop counting the bundles. "Listen, Jean-Claude," she said, "life is like the river. It has to be made up of salty currents as well as fresh. Think of how happy we'll be when we meet here again."

At last the boy let Memère loose. But he stood sobbing beside his mother while the others helped load the boxes and bundles. The conductor grumbled that some of them should have been checked for the baggage car. Memère sharply told him that she was not going to trust a single possession out of her sight. Then she and Pepère kissed everyone good-bye.

Now it was Memère's turn to weep. "God bless you all," she sobbed. Her most important blessing was for Maman. "And may the good God give you the health and patience to raise your children," she said in a trembling voice, as if she didn't expect to see her for many years.

The whistle blew impatiently. The conductor sternly urged the grandparents up the steps. The big wheels began to turn and the train moved—slowly, faster, fast. It had to reach Quebec at a certain time or all the timetables would be wrong.

The family silently rode back to the ferry dock and now Gabie could sit on the seat with Papa and Maman and Bébé.

Jean-Claude crouched on the floor with his cheeks between his hands and his eyes downcast. He wished he were a white whale playing in the river. He wished he were a little dog chasing sheep. He wished Jeanette had pushed the wagon off the plank and drowned him. He mostly wished that Monsieur Morin had left his house to somebody else.

Then as he dismally looked about the bed of the wagon, he saw something under the seat.

"The boots, Papa," he cried. "Pepère's boots with the rubbers in them."

It was a matter for regret and for trying to place the blame. Jean-Claude said nothing because he suddenly remembered that his weeping had interrupted Memère when she was counting the bundles. He pulled the boots into his lap and held them all the way home.

"Perhaps they will come back for them," he said hopefully.

Papa flicked the lines. "I do not think they will ever return," he stated. "I think my mother will stay on her own island."

CHAPTER SEVEN

When they were home again, Jean-Claude carried the boots down to his grandparents' house. He sat down on the steps and waited for them to return for the boots. He would squeeze his eyelids tightly, then spring them open, hoping to see Memère and Pepère coming up the lane.

At last he sighed deeply, then went to the mill. It looked very lonely with its long arms pegged. He went inside and climbed the steps to the upper story. The white cat followed him like a ghost.

Jean-Claude swept the floor, although there were few sweepings to gather. The white cat looked at him questioningly, then ran over to the brake and clawed it.

"No, Minou, no grinding today," said Jean-Claude. "They've left us all alone."

He climbed to his favorite nook in the window and looked to see if the ferry was in sight. Of course he couldn't expect Memère and Pepère until the ferry brought them back. He watched a great ocean liner sail down the channel. Jean-Claude wondered if Memère and Pepère were on it. He hoped they weren't.

At last he grew restless and jumped down. He gathered the white cat into his arms. "Come, Minou," he said. "They won't be able to come back until tomorrow. They'll have to get off that train and take another one back."

He met Michel in the lane. His brother was leading La Blanchet to their barn. The brown horse didn't want to go. She kept stopping and turning her head toward the mill.

"Perhaps we shouldn't take them home yet, Mich'," said Jean-Claude. "Perhaps Memère and Pepère will change their minds and come back tonight."

Michel jerked at La Blanchet's halter. "Jean-Claude," he said, "you are foolish as a broom. You know they won't change their minds when they've already bought their tickets."

La Blanchet was coaxed into the barn and put in the stall next to Jeanette. She slumped on her hind leg and sulked. Jean-Claude put the cat down.

"This is your home now," he said. "You must keep the rats away."

The family was very silent at supper that night.

"Eat your potatoes, Jean-Claude," said Maman, "and stop looking so far away."

After supper, when the sun was low over the Laurentians, Jean-Claude went to his grandparents' place again. He had an idea in his well-made head. He would light a lantern and set it in the window of the mill so the grandparents could see it from their big ship if they sailed during the night. They would know that Jean-Claude was thinking of them and wanting them back.

At the mill door he jumped in fright as something bounded past him. It was Minou. The cat had returned to the mill too. Jean-Claude left the door open so that he could see by the fading light. He found a torn sack and made a bed for Minou.

Then he climbed the steps, and by the last rays of the sun coming through the window, he found Pepère's lantern which was used when he ground during the night. The boy fished a match from the glass jar in which the matches were kept so mice wouldn't nibble them and start a fire. He raised the lantern's chimney and struck the match against the wall. When the wick was lit, it smoked badly so he had to turn it lower. At last he had the lantern burning with a steady light so he carefully set it in the window niche.

Jean-Claude stood by the window for a long while. He watched the sun sink behind the Laurentians. He watched the river turn from blue to silver to black. He reluctantly left the mill and went home.

When he said his night prayers, he added a new one. Memère and Pepère had strong wills of their own so if the good God couldn't coax them back immediately, would He please take care of them wherever they were?

It was in the middle of the night and all the Plouffes were sleeping soundly when the pounding on the door began. Jean-Claude woke up before Michel. He could hear the excited voices below. He shook his brother. "Wake up, Mich'," he cried joyfully. "Memère and Pepère have come back for the boots."

Jean-Claude hurried down the stairs. But it wasn't Memère and Pepère at the door. It was Monsieur Roy in his nightshirt with his wife's straw hat on his head. Papa was standing at the door in his nightshirt with his jacket over his shoulders, and Maman was getting into her cotton wrapper.

"The mill's on fire!" cried Monsieur Roy. "Your father's mill is on fire!"

He and Papa went running down the lane. Maman quickly grabbed the water pail. "Stay home with Bébé," she cried over her shoulder to Gabie. "The mill's on fire. Somebody must stay with Bébé."

As she ran after the others, the water sloshed over her wrapper. Michel and Jean-Claude soon caught up with the men.

"My Oliva saw it," panted Monsieur Roy. "He was coming home from courting the Boulet girl and he saw the fire in the mill."

"Wait for me," wailed Maman, all out of breath. "Wait for me."

But no one paid any attention to her. Everybody tried to open the door of the mill at the same time, so that delayed them enough for Maman to reach them.

At last Papa swung the door open. Firelight showed through the cracks above. Maman in her excitement threw

the water. It drenched Papa as he made for the steps, but he didn't even feel it.

He reached the upper story in a couple of bounds, then stopped in surprise. "It's a lantern," he said. "There's a lantern burning in the window."

They all stood staring foolishly at the lantern—Monsieur Roy with his wife's hat on his head, Papa looking as if he were wearing a short skirt under his jacket, and Maman still clutching the empty pail.

Monsieur Roy began to apologize. "My son knew that your parents were gone," he said, "so naturally he mistook a light in the mill for fire. And as you know, a young man in love does not have all his wits."

"Who lit the lantern and put it there?" asked Michel.

Slowly all the eyes turned upon Jean-Claude who wished he had stayed home with Bébé.

"Jean-Claude," growled Papa, "who lit the lantern?"

The white cat purred and rubbed its coat against the boy's bare leg.

"Minou didn't stay in our barn, Papa," said the boy. "I guess he got homesick."

"Don't stand there and tell me that Minou lit the lantern," roared his father.

Jean-Claude scraped his big toe against the floor. "No, Papa," he said miserably. "Minou can't light a lantern. Danielle's little dog can pull a wagon, but even he couldn't light a lantern."

Papa pointed his finger at the boy. "Jean-Claude," he shouted fiercely, "did you light that lantern?"

"Yes, Papa," answered the boy, shivering in his thin nightshirt. "Minou didn't do it. I did."

Papa was dripping on the floor. He was beginning to

realize that Maman had thrown the water on him to put out a fire that wasn't there. He began to shiver too. Reaching over quickly, he grabbed Jean-Claude by the shoulders and began to shake him. He shook him and shook him until the boy felt as if he were in Maman's butter churn. When Jean-Claude thought he would surely turn into butter, Papa set him free.

Then Papa apologized to Monsieur Roy for having been brought out of bed in the middle of the night because his naughty son had lit a lantern in the mill. Monsieur Roy apologized to Papa and Maman for getting them out of their beds in the middle of the night because his lovesick son had mistaken the lantern for a fire. Maman gave Jean-Claude her own scolding. "After all," she said, "it would have been a real fire if Minou had knocked the lantern over during the night."

They filed down the steps to the roundhouse. As they stepped outside, Oliva Roy came galloping up in a cart filled with tubs of water.

"There is no fire," his father told him. "It was only a lantern burning in the mill. You can go to bed and dream about Claire."

Jean-Claude thought that Monsieur Roy should have

given his son a good shaking too. He still felt a little shaken the next day when he went back to the grandparents' house with his nightshirt in his wagon.

"I'm going to live here until Merère gets back," he told the chickens. "Those people across the road don't want me in their family."

He went inside and looked at Memère's rocking chair. He sat on the floor beside it. He gave it a push so that it slowly rocked back and forth as if Memère were sitting in it.

"You should have taken me with you," he said to the chair. "If you hadn't gone away, all this wouldn't have happened." There was no voice from the chair. Jean-Claude imagined one. He imagined it saying, "Listen, Jean-Claude, it is all their fault. Your family doesn't understand you." Jean-Claude felt better. He rocked the chair some more.

Then the voice of his conscience began speaking to him. "It was not all their fault, Jean-Claude," said the small voice. "Most of it was yours because you should not have lit the lantern without asking your Papa about it."

Jean-Claude got up from the floor. He would give his family another chance, as Memère used to say.

When he returned home, no one seemed to be angry with him. Papa politely invited him to help pull weeds in the garden. He even called him a good little worker. Maman gave him an extra piece of cake at dinner, and Michel showed him how to make bits of paper cling to a comb by rubbing the comb on the hooked rug first.

And that night when Jean-Claude started toward the stairs, Papa winked at him and said, "I hope the mill doesn't catch on fire tonight and get old Jules Roy out in his wife's hat again." Then Papa leaned back in his chair and laughed so uproariously that the chair nearly went over backward. Jean-Claude smiled crookedly because he wasn't sure whether that was funny or not.

CHAPTER EIGHT

The Plouffes counted the days as they followed each other on the kitchen calendar. *Lundi, mardi, mercredi, jeudi*—.

"They must be halfway across the ocean by now."

"They should be arriving in France today."

"Will the ship take them straight to the Ile de Ré?"

"Of course not, Jean-Claude. First they must arrive at the seaport of Le Havre. Then they must go to Paris. Then they must catch a train to La Rochelle." Since it was vacation time, when Jean-Claude wasn't helping his father with the farm chores he was sitting on the grandparents' porch like a watchdog. He was guarding their possessions, and he was waiting for their return.

Then one wonderful day, the first letter arrived from France. Papa would not open it until all the family was gathered around him. Jean-Claude felt that he would burst or die waiting for Michel to come in from the barn.

Papa read the letter slowly because Memère's handwriting was so fine and the paper so thin.

They had had a good trip over except that Pepère, the old sailor, had been seasick. Ha! Ha!

"It was probably from all the excitement," put in Maman.

"No," said Papa. "I think that perhaps he ate too much. I remember that the meals were included in the fare, so naturally my father ate like an ogre."

"I think it was the thick seas," said Michel. "It must have been windy. Only last Tuesday Oliva Roy was seasick in his canoe because the wind made the water thick."

Jean-Claude squeezed his father's arm. "Please read on, Papa," he begged. "When are they coming home?"

Memère wrote that her island had changed little, although there were more tourists nowadays. But the sandy beaches were the same, and the marshes were as wet as ever. And the windmills were still there although they were no longer in use, which Pepère felt was a great waste of mill and wind. "It reminds me very much of your island," she wrote.

"The ferry must be larger if they have so many tourists," said Maman. "I wonder how many passengers it carries."

"Why should it be larger?" demanded Papa. "Our ferry is large enough to carry fifty passengers if they don't bring their horses and wagons with them."

"Oh, no, Papa," interrupted Michel. "It isn't allowed to carry that many. There aren't enough life jackets."

Jean-Claude squeezed his father's arm. "When are they coming back?" he asked. "Does the letter say?"

Papa cleared his throat and went on with the letter. Marianne was well and had twenty-one lively grandchildren to keep her company. Ha! Ha! They all sent their love.

"Twenty-one grandchildren," put in Gabie disdainfully. "Madame Lacour has sixty."

"And the old Boulets have over a hundred great-grandchildren," added Maman.

The letter had an important message for Papa. "That stupid conductor hurried us so when we reached Quebec that our boots were left behind on the train," wrote

Memère. "Will you please go to the railroad station the first time you cross the river, and ask if the boots have been found?"

There was no "Ha! Ha!" about the boots.

The letter ended with love and kisses and hugs, but no mention of their return.

"When are they coming back?" persisted Jean-Claude. "Why didn't Memère say anything about it?"

"They have just arrived," said Maman, "so naturally they aren't thinking of coming back right away."

Papa returned the pages to the envelope. Then he stared into space and lightly tapped a little rhythm against the envelope.

"May I have the stamp on the envelope?" asked Michel.

Papa slowly tore it off for him. "No, I don't think my parents will return to Canada," he said. Jean-Claude felt as if he had fallen into the St. Lawrence. Life would be that dark and cold without Memère and Pepère. Papa thoughtfully blew through his mustache. "So I might as well go ahead and buy the red tractor," he decided.

Jean-Claude felt lifted from the deep, dark waters of despair. The red tractor! How wonderful it would be to have it on their farm. He could hardly wait to tell the other boys about it. But his spirits dropped again.

"I would rather have Memère and Pepère than the tractor, Papa," he said.

Papa tried to reason with him. "My little man," he said, "we are not trading Memère and Pepère for a tractor. They are not coming back to our island. Was it mentioned in the letter? Naturally I will go ahead and buy the tractor since I have no father here to advise me about it."

"But I *know* they're coming back," insisted Jean-Claude. "Memère didn't take her rocking chair."

"Now, my little one," said Maman, "it is not polite to correct your father. If Papa says they are not coming back, *eh bien,* they are not coming back."

When Papa sat down at the table with a pencil and tablet that night, the boy asked, "Are you writing to ask Pepère about the tractor?"

Papa stopped writing. "Jean-Claude," he said, "would I worry my father about a tractor when he is so busy on the Ile de Ré? He is probably running one of those windmills by now."

"Will you ask him if he is ever coming back?" asked the boy timidly.

Papa began erasing. "*Zut,* you made me misspell a

word," he said. "I am not writing to my father at all. I am writing to the agent across the river about the red tractor."

Maman came to the table and leaned over Papa's shoulder. She read his words. She clapped her hands. "Now we will no longer be as poor as Goodman Job." She smiled. "We will have a modern farm."

"I only hope it gets here in time for the harvest," said Papa.

He finished the letter, writing his Jean-Baptiste Plouffe with large capitals and long wavy tails that underlined each name.

Then Papa and Maman became quite gay. They began singing their happy song. It was an old French song which they sang in turns. All through it, Maman pretended to be running away from Papa.

"If you shall come Sunday, I'll not be there," Maman trilled. "I'll turn myself into a doe."

Then Papa sang that if she turned into a doe, he would become a hunter and chase her. But no, Maman fooled him, because if he became a hunter, she would turn into a carp in a brook. Papa took a deep breath and rolled his brown eyes. If she did that, he would become a fisherman so he could catch her. And so the song went with Maman and Papa changing their forms with each verse.

Jean-Claude couldn't help being happy, too, when Maman and Papa sang that song. Tonight he took his alder flute and played the tune with secret words in his well-made head. If Memère didn't come back soon, he would become a white whale and follow her across the sea. If she then turned into a white goose, he would turn into a hawk and chase her. If she turned into a sea pink, he would become a little frog and find her in the marsh.

His secret song was ended by his surprise. Papa was chasing Maman around the kitchen table. Twice he chased her around it until he caught her near the woodbox and gave her a loud kiss.

Jean-Claude was astonished at his parents' behaviour. Then quick as a breeze he realized it was because they were so happy. It was because they had wanted the tractor so much all the time Pepère had been against it.

For two whole weeks Jean-Claude stopped asking when Pepère and Memère would get back. He didn't want them to return until Papa had the tractor.

Instead he would ask each day, "When is the tractor

coming, Papa?" One time when he was in the tool shed with his father, he asked, "What will you do if the tractor doesn't come in time for the harvest?"

Papa was busy mixing Paris green with water in the big watering can. He was going to spray "the little beasts," as he called the insects on the plants.

"That will be my problem," answered Papa sternly. "You have enough problems of your own to worry about, little man. And the first one I want you to worry about are those raspberry bushes you pulled up by the roots—the ones I set out so carefully last spring. What about them?"

Jean-Claude lowered his eyes guiltily. He felt like one of the little beasts on the plants. "I wanted to see if the roots had taken a good hold yet," he tried to explain about the bushes. "I am going to be a farmer when I grow up."

"Oh, no, Jean-Claude," corrected his father. "You are not going to be a farmer if you pull up young berry bushes."

"I will put them back in the ground, Papa," offered the boy. "I like to dig holes."

"They are dead now," said Papa, "but you can get the small shovel and begin digging a hole for the new post I am going to set for a gate to the pasture."

"Yes, Papa," said Jean-Claude obediently, although he really didn't like to dig holes that well.

He went toward the pasture and moved the rock Papa

had placed on the ground to show where the gate post should be. He began digging. The afternoon sun was hot on his back. The ground was hard and dry. Then his well-made head began thinking that there might be some other way to make amends for the raspberry bushes. Perhaps he could go out in the woods and dig up something to replace them. Why not a wild cherry tree? No one else on the island ever planted a wild cherry tree in his orchard. Apple trees, plum trees, and all kinds of tame trees. A wild cherry would be a change. Jean-Claude liked to eat the tiny red berries in the late summer. They had a tart taste that always surprised his tongue. And Maman could make jelly from them—if he left any.

As he thought about this his shovel struck a stubborn stone. Jean-Claude decided that Maman really needed a wild cherry tree.

CHAPTER NINE

Jean-Claude dragged the shovel with one hand as he pushed through the thicket at the edge of the road. His other gripped a wild cherry sapling. It wasn't any bigger than a switch and some of the roots had been torn off, but it had cost him quite a struggle. That is why some of the leaves had been pulled off too. He couldn't understand how such a small tree could have so many long roots. Surely if the raspberry bushes had had such roots, they never would have responded to his tugging.

He stood at the edge of the road and laid the shovel down so he could wipe his scratched, sweating face.

As he took the shovel up again, he saw a lumbering object off in the distance. He waited for it to draw closer. Yes, it was the Boulets' oxcart. On the seat were hunched Jacques and Pichou Boulet, always together like two drops of water.

Jean-Claude waved the cherry switch at them, then he began running toward the approaching oxen.

"May I ride with you?" he panted. "Please give me a ride on the oxcart."

He had always yearned for a ride on the slow-moving

cart to the stout oxen's steady pull, but the Boulet boys had never given him that treat. They were Michel's friends and if anyone got a ride, it was Michel.

"We have no time to fool with you," grumbled Jacques. "We're in a hurry."

"Oh, let's give the little chick a ride," said Pichou. "He's always begging for one."

He obligingly stopped the red and white team. Jacques reached for the shovel and threw it into the cart. Then he swung Jean-Claude up. The big boys moved apart so Jean-Claude could sit between them.

Pichou prodded the oxen with the goad. *"Huhau!"* he shouted. The beasts stretched at their wooden yoke and the cart majestically moved on.

Jean-Claude wished his parents had a team of oxen instead of Jeanette. He watched their strong neck muscles swell against the heavy yoke. He heard their cloven hoofs thudding in the dust. He watched the coarse tassels on their tails sway from side to side with each step. The chains jingled faintly.

Then a rumbling sound far behind made all three boys turn their heads. A large truck was bearing down upon them.

"Somebody from the mainland," said Pichou. "They're always in such a big hurry."

"Let's slow them down," suggested Jacques.

"Dia! Dia!" cried Pichou, giving each ox a poke with the goad. The obedient beasts turned left and continued down the middle of the road. The truck roared up to them. Its driver hung his head out of the cab and cupped his mouth.

"Hé!" he shouted. "Can you tell me the way to Jean-Baptiste Plouffe's farm? I'm bringing him a tractor."

Jean-Claude excitedly jumped to his feet. But before he could utter a word, Jacques jerked him back to the seat. "Sit down, little chick," he ordered. "You asked for an oxcart ride, didn't you?"

"But I don't want one now," protested Jean-Claude.

Pichou jabbed the boy in the ribs. "Sit still and stop clacking your beak," he commanded. Then he winked at his brother before turning around. "Just follow us," he shouted back. Both Boulet boys began to giggle.

The oxcart crept over the dusty road. The truck jerked behind in its slowest gear. Jean-Claude felt like an eel in a river trap.

Then the driver honked his horn. "Can't one of you boys get in with me and show me the way?" he suggested.

Jean-Claude tried to rise, but Pichou held him down. At the same time, the older boy called back, "No, we have to drive the oxen."

"I can go with him," persisted Jean-Claude.

"No, you can't," retorted Jacques. "You have to take an oxcart ride. You wanted one, didn't you?"

Jean-Claude nodded miserably. He puzzled over the fact that an oxcart ride which had seemed so wonderful a few minutes ago could become such torture. Jacques and Pichou bent over and shook with more giggles. From time to time they would sneak backward glances at the snorting truck.

Its driver honked again. "If you'll just tell me how to get there," he called, "I'll go on ahead."

Pichou called back, "It's very hard to find. You might get lost. Follow us."

Jean-Claude was frozen to the seat with his fear. Perhaps the man would suspect that the boys were teasing him. Perhaps he would turn around and take the tractor back to the mainland.

Another squawking honk came from the truck. "My faith," cried the man, "can't your oxen go any faster?"

"I don't know, monsieur," returned Pichou truthfully. "They never have."

Jean-Claude's tight muscles loosened. The turnoff for his house was only a few slow ox steps ahead. To his unhappy surprise, the oxen went past it without being halted by Pichou.

"You're passing it," cried Jean-Claude. "That's our lane."

Pichou stopped giggling to frown at him. "You asked for a ride in an oxcart," he glowered, "so you're going to get a good long one. Aren't you ever satisfied?"

Tears came into Jean-Claude's eyes and his lower lip trembled. Now Papa would never get his red tractor.

When they reached the roadside cross, Pichou stopped the oxen. Then he turned to the truck driver. "Why are you still following us? The Plouffe farm is back there," he pointed.

They could see the driver's mouth opening and closing angrily. They could hear the grinding of the gears as he savagely jerked his truck backward.

"Now you may get down, my little chick," Pichou told

Jean-Claude, "and when you see Mich', tell him we gave you that ride you were always begging for."

Jacques tossed the shovel to the ground. As Jean-Claude stooped to pick it up the truck backed into a field to make the turn. With his shovel dragging in the dirt and the cherry switch still clutched in his hand, the boy raced toward the truck.

"I'll go with you and show you the Plouffe farm," shouted Jean-Claude.

The driver scowled at him. "I've had enough help from you stupid *habitants*," he retorted. Then the truck leaped away, blinding Jean-Claude with its cloud of dust. But to the boy's giddy delight, when he was able to open his eyes he saw the big truck turning into his father's lane. And riding in back of it was a bright red tractor.

Jean-Claude ran up the lane through the dust made by the truck from the mainland. Papa was already coming from the garden to meet it. Michel was following him. Maman stood at the kitchen door, drying her hands on her apron. Beside her was Gabie holding a dishtowel.

All the Plouffes made big eyes at the beautiful red tractor with its giant rear wheels.

"Good day, monsieur." Papa bowed to the truck driver

as if he were a guest coming for dinner. "I see that you have brought the new member of my family."

The truck driver was not so gay as the others, but he touched the brim of his greasy cap politely. "Are you Jean-Baptiste Plouffe?" he asked.

Papa was so happy that he became playful with Maman again. "Ah, my good wife." He winked at her. "Am I Jean-Baptiste Plouffe or did you marry the wrong man?"

"And I'm Jean-Claude Plouffe," put in the little boy eagerly, because he wanted the driver to know that some of the red tractor belonged to him too.

The man heavily climbed down from the cab of the truck and walked to the back of it. He had a rolling gait which came from riding in a truck cab all day, not from walking the deck of a ship.

"So you are Jean-Claude Plouffe," he said drily to the excited boy. "I think we have met before."

"I was in the oxcart," said Jean-Claude. He looked toward his father. "What is a *habitant*?" he asked him.

"He is a man of the country," replied Papa. "He is a man who works the soil on which he lives, and he owes homage to no one. I am a *habitant*," he finished proudly.

"Ah, yes, yes," put in the truck driver quickly. "A fine,

worthy fellow is the *habitant*. He is the backbone of our province of Quebec. Now wouldn't you like to help us unload the tractor, my little fellow?"

The tailgate of the truck made a ramp so that the tractor could be slowly rolled down it by the aid of ropes. Jean-Claude really was no help, but it wasn't because he didn't try. As soon as the tractor was safe on the ground, he began pulling at the levers.

"What makes it go?" he asked the driver.

"Your father can explain all of that to you," said the man, twisting his greasy cap on his head impatiently. "I must hurry or I will miss the ferry back."

Papa looked at him blankly. "How *does* it run?" he asked. "I have never driven a tractor."

The truck driver edged toward his cab. "It drives just like an automobile," he said. "You have the gears and the brake. Of course you have to start it by hand."

Papa's face looked blanker than ever. "My wagon has a brake," he said, "but no gears. I do not know what they are. I have never driven an automobile."

The truck driver looked at Papa as if he were a little boy. "But surely you have driven something mechanical," he said.

Papa shook his head sadly. "I have never driven anything but horses," he said.

Jean-Claude wrinkled his forehead wonderingly, as if he were trying to put two and two together. Then he asked, "Papa, are there any stupid *habitants*?"

The driver took Papa's attention as fast as he could. "There is nothing to worry about," he assured him. "I have a booklet that goes with the tractor. It will give you all the instructions." He slouched from side to side as he went to the cab and picked out the booklet.

Papa signed some papers, then the truck hurriedly backed down the lane. The Plouffes were alone with their new tractor.

"Will we cultivate the potato plants today?" asked Jean-Claude.

"Yes, indeed," replied his father. "As soon as I have read this booklet, we will hitch the cultivator to the tractor and run it over the potatoes."

Jean-Claude climbed into the saddle seat of the tractor and pretended that he was driving it. Maman kept walking around it and admiring it from all directions. Gabie brought Bébé out to see it. Papa sat down on the kitchen steps and began to read the booklet with Michel squinting over his shoulder.

"Hand-crank starting . . . differential . . . power take-off—simple for even a small boy or woman to operate," he slowly read. Then Papa scowled and threw the booklet on the steps. "Can you operate this gasoline machine, Michel?" he cried. "You, Jean-Claude?"

Both boys shook their heads. "Pierre Gignac has a tractor," said Michel. "He will probably teach you how to drive it."

"This booklet does not say that Pierre Gignac will teach me to drive the tractor," stormed Papa. "It says that even a woman can operate it. Can you, Marie?" he demanded of Maman.

"I can drive a horse and push a baby carriage," said Maman. "That is all I need to know."

Jean-Claude was not discouraged. "I will try to drive it, Papa," he cried. He began pulling and pushing levers. He turned the wheel one way and then the other. "*Giouac!*" he shouted, as if the tractor were a horse. "*Huhau!*" he cried, as if the tractor were an ox.

Papa had to laugh and Maman joined him. "We will

have to wait until Pierre Gignac comes over to teach me," Papa finally admitted.

"Won't we be able to cultivate the potatoes this afternoon?" Jean-Claude asked anxiously.

"Why can't you hitch Jeanette to the tractor and have her pull it?" suggested Maman brightly.

Papa looked at her as if she had no more sense than Bébé. "My good wife," he said, "we bought this tractor to take Jeanette's *place.* As soon as I learn how to drive it, we will sell the horse. There are thirty horses in this machine—if I can only learn how to drive them."

At dusk Pierre Gignac walked over to the Plouffe farm at Michel's request. He patiently taught Papa how to drive the new tractor with the thirty horses hidden under its red hood. It had been a long time since Papa had gone to school, but he applied himself well and learned quickly. When at last he was able to steer the tractor and back it up successfully, he grinned sheepishly. "*Alors,* it's so simple that even a child or woman could operate it," he beamed.

That night at supper, Papa was happy as a king. "I am no stupid *habitant,* I can tell you," he announced. "I am now a modern farmer. *Adieu* to Jeanette. She was a faithful, hardworking beast but she is too old-fashioned for Jean-Baptiste Plouffe. Perhaps we should sell La Blanchet for my father too."

But after they had said grace, Maman asked, "How will we get to church without Jeanette? How will we shop in the village? All of us can't ride on the tractor."

At first Papa considered using the tractor to pull the cart, then he realized that was not sensible. "It would be as foolish as having Jeanette pull the tractor," he admitted. He forked a cold potato and twirled it around thoughtfully. "No," he said, "the tractor is equal to thirty horses, so what difference does one more make? We will keep Jeanette and own thirty-one horses. But I must sell La Blanchet."

CHAPTER TEN

The red tractor lived up to its promise. It cultivated and mowed and hauled while Jeanette and La Blanchet grew fat in the barnyard. It even took Jean-Claude for a ride from the pasture to the backyard. Of course he had to sit on Papa's lap, but Papa let him steer the wheel.

"May I drive the tractor all by myself?" begged the boy.

"No, no, my little man," said Papa. "You will have to wait until you grow up."

"I wish I were a big man like you, Papa," said Jean-Claude wistfully.

"*Là! là!* Don't be in such a hurry to pile the years on your back," said Papa. "They make a heavy load."

Papa's words puzzled Jean-Claude. If only Memère were here, she could explain them to him.

"Don't you think Memère will ever come back to us?" he asked his father.

Papa brought the tractor to a stop near the barn. "My boy, we have not even heard from her in weeks," he said. "She never mentioned trying to sell the house in any of her letters. I think she plans to stay in it."

"But she didn't say she *wasn't* coming back," persisted the boy.

He wished the grandparents could see the new tractor. He wished they could see him driving it. Then Pepère would be happy that Papa had bought the gasoline machine, as he had called it.

"I think now that I have the tractor out, I might as well mow those weeds along the lane," said Papa. "They will make good forage for the horses. *Hé!* I must get that Blanchet sold. With gasoline to buy for this red one, I can't be feeding two horses also."

Jean-Claude hated the thought of selling La Blanchet. It would be like cutting another bond with his grandparents.

Papa left the tractor running while he went into the

shed to get the mowing blade. Jean-Claude hopped back into the seat. He pretended that he was driving the machine for Pepère. He turned the wheel from one side to the other. He touched different levers in turn. It began to seem very real to him. He pulled the brake. He pressed his foot here as he had seen Papa do so often. He pulled the lever there.

The tractor began to move. When Jean-Claude looked up, he saw the house coming to him. With a scream, he turned the wheel and the house turned away also.

"Papa! Papa!" screamed Jean-Claude. "Help! Help!"

Papa came running from the shed. "Pull the brake!" he cried. "The brake!"

But Jean-Claude didn't have time to pull the brake because the tractor was turning toward the barn.

The screams and shouts brought Maman from the garden where she had been gathering rhubarb.

"Jump off!" cried Maman in terror, waving a stalk of rhubarb at Jean-Claude.

"No! No!" cried Papa, trying to catch up with the tractor. "You'll fall under the wheels. Pull the brake!"

"To the right," cried Maman because the tractor was headed for the hen house. "Jump off!"

"To the left," shouted Papa because the tractor was now going toward the fence. "Hold on tight. Pull the brake!"

Jean-Claude was so frightened that he clung to the wheel with all his might. He felt as helpless as if he were really driving thirty horses. He tried to stop the tractor by pulling back on the wheel. *"Hoa! Hoa!"* he shouted to the thirty horses.

Then the tractor crashed into the side of the house and obediently stopped of its own accord. Jean-Claude shakily let go of the wheel and climbed down.

Papa and Maman raced to him. "Are you hurt, my child?" cried Maman with tears in her eyes.

Papa anxiously brushed Maman aside. He felt Jean-Claude's head all over to see that it wasn't cracked. He made the boy move his arms and legs and wiggle his fingers and toes. He poked his backbone. Jean-Claude was unharmed.

Then Papa went to the tractor and looked at it. The tractor had not fared as well as its driver. It was crushed against the wall of the house.

Papa's face began to swell and grow as red as flannelet. He glared fiercely at Jean-Claude. His black mustache

lowered over his clenched teeth. He grabbed Jean-Claude, pulled him over his knee and gave him such a spanking that the boy thought he would surely burst open like an overripe tomato. The spanking stung all the way to his bones.

Then Papa stood him up and finished the spanking with a shaking. "Jean-Claude," shouted Papa, "you have broken the tractor. Now what are we going to do?"

Jean-Claude didn't know. He could only weep into his hands. *Boo, hoo, hoo!* He hadn't meant to break the tractor. *Bou, hou, hou!* He really hadn't even meant to drive it. *Bou, hou, hou!*

Maman sat down on the porch steps and cried too. Jean-Claude was sure that she was crying about the tractor and not about his spanking.

"What gets into you?" Michel asked Jean-Claude in disgust. He had heard the commotion all the way out in the potato field and had come running.

"It is probably the Devil," put in Gabie, who was also present by this time. "It must be. Sometimes he is good as wheat."

So Gabie got the little bottle from the kitchen shelf and sprinkled Jean-Claude with holy water to get rid of the Devil in him.

The boy shook with a few more sobs, then he began to hiccough. *Hoquet! Hoquet!* Maman gave him a sip of the holy water. At last Jean-Claude was over the *hoquets*. "What will Papa do about the tractor?" he asked.

"What can I do but send it to the garage on the mainland to have it repaired?" Papa asked savagely. "And that will cost a good many bags of potatoes."

And how would the broken tractor get to the mainland? Papa solved that problem. "It is so heavy that I will have to team up Jeanette and La Blanchet and let them pull it there," he said. "They will have something to do beside eating their heads off. It is a good thing I have not sold La Blanchet yet. Perhaps I should keep her too."

Jean-Claude watched Papa and Michel as they wound chains around the tractor. "Can I help you?" he asked contritely.

"You have helped me enough already," said Papa huffily. "I don't want you even to breathe on this tractor again."

Michel led the horses down the lane. Papa sat on the tractor and steered the wheel. Slowly the strange procession disappeared down the road.

Jean-Claude did not pack up his nightshirt and go to

the grandparents' house. Not even that could comfort him. He would have to do something more daring. Perhaps he should run away. That was a good idea. He would run away to the mainland and take a ship to the Ile de Ré. He would run away to his grandparents since they weren't coming back to his island.

But when he went through the kitchen at the very beginning of his journey, a wonderful smell filled his nose.

"What are you cooking?" Jean-Claude asked his mother.

"I'm baking rhubarb pies," Maman told him.

But that was all she said because she was angry with Jean-Claude too.

Despite Maman's manner, the boy decided to wait to eat a piece of pie before he ran away.

The rhubarb pie was unusually good. Maman had tried putting a little cinnamon in the crust to see what that would do. It did something splendid.

There were still two pies left for the next day, so Jean-Claude decided he would wait until the pies were all gone before he ran away.

Although everyone still treated him coldly, the boy gave up the idea of running away. He had thought of something better. While taking the cow to and from the pasture, he had noticed a hornets' nest swinging from a tree. It looked like a huge gray ball, and Jean-Claude had often wished he could get it away from the hornets and have it for his plaything.

If he were badly stung by the hornets, everyone would love him again. Memère had often said that there was nothing like sickness to draw a family close together. Even when he had wrecked the tractor, Papa and Maman had thought of his safety first.

He would knock the nest down with a stick and the angry hornets would sting him. He would be red and swollen and sick. Then everyone would forgive him for the tractor affair. And when he was well, he could go back and get the hornets' nest for his ball.

Jean-Claude set out after the nest. It occurred to him that it hung so high he would need a very long stick. He didn't know where he would find one. Then he thought that a pitchfork would be perfect.

He made for the barn. He opened the door and stepped inside. His plan was ruined. Papa was in the barn using the pitchfork.

"I am pushing the old hay aside to make room for a new load," said Papa. "What do you want, Jean-Claude?"

Jean-Claude stood hesitantly by the door. The barn was almost in twilight because there was only one small window under each gable.

The pigeons were softly cooing under the thatched roof. In their stalls, the horses snuffled at their mangers. It was very peaceful in the old barn.

Suddenly words came to Jean-Claude's tongue. "I'm sorry I broke the tractor, Papa," he said in a low voice.

Papa drove the pitchfork into a bale of hay. "And I'm sorry I had to spank you," apologized Papa. He sat down on the bale and beckoned to the boy. "Come here, my little one," he said. "I want to talk to you."

He pulled Jean-Claude up on his lap.

"I didn't mean to break the tractor," said the boy. "I wanted to be a big man and drive it."

"That is your trouble," said Papa. "You are still a little boy, and when you try to be big it only gets you into mischief."

"But I want to be a farmer when I am big," insisted Jean-Claude. "I want to be a farmer like you."

"And so you shall," promised Papa. "This farm will belong to you and Michel some day. Yes, one day when Maman and I are old, we shall all dress in our best clothes

—as if we are going to church. But instead, we shall go to the notary's office on the mainland and sign papers. The papers will say that the farm belongs to you and Michel. They will say that in return you are to take care of us until we die. They will also say that you are to provide for your sisters until they marry. Then all of us will sign those papers—and half of the farm will be yours."

While Jean-Claude sat on Papa's lap in the peaceful barn and listened to his earnest words, he felt very close to his father. The strange feeling came over him that he really had never known Papa very well before. It was as if the good God had taken up one of the little wooden figures and skillfully carved some more details. It was as if He had set it down beside Jean-Claude saying, "Now you will be able to see your father better."

"I wish I were a big man now." Jean-Claude sighed, laying his head against his father's shoulder.

"Do not hurry the years, little Jean-Claude," said Papa. "Remember that they are pushing Maman and me along at the same time."

Jean-Claude hated to think of his father and mother growing old like Pepère and Memère. He decided to be a little boy a while longer. He also decided to let the hornets' nest alone.

CHAPTER ELEVEN

Jean-Claude kept asking Papa when the tractor would be fixed and returned to the farm. He wondered if it would be brought back in the big truck as it had arrived the first time. He wondered if Papa himself would go and drive the tractor back on its own big wheels.

"Don't be in such a rush for the tractor to be fixed," grumbled his father. "It will only mean another big bill to be paid. Soon I will have nothing but the Devil left in my purse."

Jean-Claude was sorry about the big bill. It was his fault because he had broken the tractor. He wished he could make some money to help Papa pay for it.

He tried to think of how he could make some money that would be all his own. Of course he couldn't earn it working on the farm. Papa thought that it was a son's duty to work on his family's farm without pay. By the same string, he couldn't expect to be paid for helping on another farm. All of the farmers on his island had sons whose duty it was to work free for their fathers.

One day he was playing "leap-sheep" in the pasture with some of his friends. One boy would crouch down and another would jump over him. That one in turn would crouch and the third boy had two "sheep" to leap. And so it went. And as Pierre Richard jumped over Jean-Claude, a bright quarter fell out of his pocket.

"Oh, oh!" cried Pierre. "I mustn't lose my quarter. A tourist gave it to me yesterday for being his guide."

Jean-Claude immediately lost interest in the game of leap-sheep. He straightened. "How did that happen?" he asked.

"I was at the ferry dock when some people from Montreal arrived in a big black car. They asked me if I would go with them and show them the places of interest. The man said that we have many old things over here."

"Did you get a ride in the big black car?" asked Jean-Claude in awe.

Pierre nodded as he pocketed his coin. "I often make money during the summer by showing tourists around," he boasted. "I go to the dock and when strange people come ashore in big cars, I offer to ride with them and show them the sights. One man from Quebec did not want to see the sights, but he gave me ten cents to get rid of me."

Jean-Claude decided to go to the ferry dock after dinner. He even washed his hands and face before he set out. He wanted to look neat for his first venture into this guide business which paid so well.

As he walked down the road, scuffing the pebbles, he thought about the sights he would show the tourists. He began talking to himself for practice.

"Yes, monsieur, we are very old on this island. We have Madame Boulet who is a hundred and three years.

"There is the Gignac house which has stood for two hundred and fifty years, and we think it will stand much longer because the Gignacs take very good care of it.

"Our church of St. Louis is very old, too. I do not remember myself when it was built. These little chapels every half mile are used during church processions, and my brother Michel marches at the head of them because he is an altar boy.

"The big cross with the white fence around it, madame? That is where the great explorer Jacques Cartier stepped ashore. That was the longest time ago.

"See that old windmill down the lane? It was built over three hundred years ago and it is still in use. That is, it will be when its owner returns from the Ile de Ré. On the other side of the road you will see the old farm where the Plouffes live. Someday their son Jean-Claude will own half of it.

"Oh, monsieur, thank you a thousand times for the quarter. It will help pay for the new tractor that Jean-Claude broke."

When Jean-Claude passed a clump of wild cherries, he was pleased to see that the fruit was red. He broke off a branch, and as he walked along he slowly picked off cherry after cherry and popped them into his mouth.

He made a face over each tart bite. He thought them even better than raw rhubarb—and certainly as good as the pickles that some of the boys bought at the village store.

He remembered the little tree he had brought home to plant for Maman. He wondered what had happened to it. Had he dropped it from the oxcart, or had he laid it down somewhere at home when they were unloading the red tractor? He made a face that had nothing to do with a wild cherry. He was remembering how he had made the tractor go *crac, boum, paf*.

As he skipped down the hill to the dock he looked across the dark blue channel of the St. Lawrence to the light blue Laurentian Mountains. He wished he could see all the way to the garage where the tractor was being repaired.

A few islanders were waiting for the ferry. All of them were staring hopefully across the channel, even Monsieur Peltrie's horses.

Jean-Claude could see the ferry far in the distance, zigzagging its way through the salty currents and the fresh ones. He hoped there would be many big fine automobiles on it.

"Would you care for a guide, monsieur? There are

many old things to be seen on this island, and I know where they are because I have lived here all my life."

He ran to the edge of the dock as the men threw the ropes to draw the ferry in. His heart sank. There were some horses and carts, but the only automobile on the ferry was a battered truck.

Jean-Claude thrust his hands into his pockets and watched the horses crossing the wide planks. Perhaps someone would give him a ride home—perhaps Madame Richard in her light cart. Then the boy's eyes opened wider and he forgot all about the guide business. Because sitting on the seat with Madame Richard were Memère and Pepère. No wonder he hadn't known them at first. They didn't look like themselves. Memère was wearing a store hat with flowers on it, and Pepère had a new suit.

Jean-Claude began to jump about like the cork on a fishing line. He leaped and twirled as excitedly as if there were a white whale on his line.

"Memère! Pepère!" he shouted.

He tried to run down the plank to meet them, but one of the ferry workers pulled him back. "Let the passengers off first," he ordered brusquely.

Memère and Pepère were almost as surprised to see Jean-

Claude. Madame Richard stopped her horse once it was ashore, and Pepère pulled Jean-Claude up into his lap. Memère kissed him and Pepère kissed him and he took turns kissing them back.

"Why didn't you tell us you were coming?" asked Jean-Claude.

"How did you know we would be on this ferry?" asked Memère, without answering his question. "Is everyone well?"

"It is lucky that I was coming back from the mainland," said Madame Richard to Jean-Claude. "Can you imagine that they expected to walk from the railroad station to the dock with all those bundles in back?"

Jean-Claude turned his head and saw the baggage piled in Madame Richard's cart. It looked as if there was more of it than when the grandparents had left.

"We wanted to surprise our family," said Memère. "Life is dull for them so much of the time that we wanted to give them some excitement."

"It's the biggest surprise I've ever had," admitted Jean-Claude. He knew it was going to be the biggest surprise that the rest of the Plouffe family ever had, too.

Pepère jiggled Jean-Claude on his knee. "Have you been a good boy?" he asked.

"Most of the time," replied the boy truthfully. "I did get a big spanking from Papa one time."

Memère exclaimed, "Your father spanked you! And what had you done to deserve it?"

"I—I," and then Jean-Claude remembered that Pepère had told Papa not to buy the tractor. He remembered how Papa had bought the tractor during Pepère's absence. Pepère was going to have a big surprise too. But he didn't want to be the one to give it to him. "I—don't remember," Jean-Claude said as he lowered his head.

"It can't have been anything very bad if you can't even remember it," said Memère.

Ah, if Memère only knew! What a surprise that was going to be for her too. Papa had bought the forbidden tractor and he, Jean-Claude, had made it go *crac, boum, paf*.

"What good will the spanking do if you can't remember why you got it?" Pepère put in.

Hélas, Pepère! The spanking had really done a great deal of good. Now Jean-Claude would never touch that tractor without his father's permission.

"Well, let us not talk about unpleasant things," said Memère. "Today must be a happy one."

Madame Richard drove her horse and cart up the Plouffes' lane. Jean-Claude jumped down first, then went running wildly from house to barn to shed and back to the house. "Memère and Pepère," he cried to the door and the walls and the fields. "They're home again."

In no time Maman and Gabie came out of the house, Papa rushed from the potato field and Michel from the barn.

They all laughed and kissed and talked at once. Michel unloaded the bundles from the cart while Papa kissed his parents and Jean-Claude raced around in circles like a little dog chasing its own tail.

"Why didn't you tell us you were coming?"

"When did you leave France?"

"When did you get to Quebec?"

All the questions were asked but not answered. The family moved up the steps and into the house, laughing and asking questions all the way. They went through the door to the parlor and as Jean-Claude pressed closely to his grandparents, someone firmly grabbed him by the straps of his overalls and pulled him back into the kitchen. It was Papa. He was acting as if he were going to tell Jean Claude a secret. He had his forefinger pressed against his mustache.

"Chut!" warned Papa. "Not one word about the tractor. It is not time to tell them about it yet. And when it is—I will be the one to do it."

Jean-Claude silently nodded. He was glad he hadn't told why he received the spanking. *Aie!* He would have to keep the bit in his mouth, and that was hard for an excitable boy to do.

Memère took the seat of honor in the rocking chair. She dropped into it as if she expected to remain there for the rest of her life.

"Ah, we had a tra-la-la trip, but it is good to be back on my island," she said.

Jean-Claude was surprised that she claimed his island as hers instead of the Ile de Ré, but it made him happy.

"Ha!" exclaimed Pepère. "Everything on Ré made her homesick for this island—the pine trees, the beaches, and the little villages."

"They are really very much alike," said Memère. "I don't know why I wasn't satisfied here."

"All islands are alike," said Pepère. "All of them are surrounded by water."

Memère smiled at Jean-Claude. "You are wrong as usual," she retorted to Pepère. "Only this island has the Plouffe family on it."

Then all of them began to talk at once and nobody listened to anyone else, but they were very happy.

"Did you bring me back anything?" Jean-Claude asked his grandmother when he could get the words in.

"For shame!" scolded Maman. "Is it polite to ask such a question?"

Jean-Claude was ashamed. "If Memère didn't bring me anything, it's all right," he apologized. "I only asked to find out."

But already Memère had hopped up from the rocking chair and was opening a suitcase. She dug deeply into it and brought out three gifts wrapped in crumpled newspapers—one for Michel, one for Gabie, and one for Jean-Claude.

"The others can wait for their presents," she explained, "because theirs are only useful things."

Jean-Claude tore the paper away. In his hand was a toy donkey wearing striped blue trousers and carrying a basket at each side. He shouted with delight. He kissed Memère and Pepère again. He made his donkey slide along the border of the carpet.

Michel's gift was a sailing ship inside a small bottle, and for Gabie there was a fluted seashell.

"If you put it to your ear," explained Memère, "you can hear the ocean at the Ile de Ré."

"And how has the farm marched this year?" Pepère asked Papa. "Do you expect a good potato crop?"

Papa gave the answer that was expected of a farmer. He complained about the weather, the "little beasts," and the cooperative stores. "But I expect a record harvest," he ended.

"Has Jean-Claude been a help?" Memère asked Maman. Jean-Claude held his breath. Maman could not always be depended upon because she often talked before she thought.

"Oh, yes," said Maman. "He has been a very good boy." Jean-Claude breathed more easily.

"Then why did you give him a spanking?" Pepère asked Papa.

"Did I give him a spanking?" asked Papa. "Ah, yes, I believe I did once."

"And what had he done?" asked Memère.

"I—well—I don't remember," said Papa. "Jean-Claude gets so many ideas in his well-made head." He looked warningly at Gabie and Michel. But it wasn't necessary because no one seemed to remember why Jean-Claude had been spanked.

"You see," cried Memère triumphantly, "I always said it did no good to spank children. One should reason with them."

Papa tried to turn the talk away from Jean-Claude. "You used to spank me when I was a boy," he reminded his mother.

"Hô!" put in Pepère. "That is because we all had good memories for why you were spanked. I remember very well the worst spanking I ever gave you myself. Remember the time I had left the horses hitched to the wagon, and you climbed up on the seat by yourself and started them?"

Memère leaned over her lap with laughter. "And they ran away and broke a wheel off the wagon," she said with tears of laughter in her eyes, "and you were thrown out!"

Jean-Claude felt better about the tractor. Perhaps the time would come when Papa and Maman would laugh that way about his breaking it. But of course, this was not that time.

CHAPTER TWELVE

In a few days it seemed as if Pepère and Memère had never been gone. They and their possessions fitted back neatly into their house. La Blanchet returned to her own stable, and the white cat was fed from his own saucer in his own mill.

Then one day Papa brought the tractor home, driving it back himself as if it were a fine big automobile. And he speeded it up the lane as fast as the thirty horses would go, with many a backward glance toward his father's house. He drove the tractor into the barn and covered its rear end with two ragged horse blankets.

"I will not really need it until harvest time," he told Maman, "so there is no hurry about telling my father that I bought it."

"Papa, how big will I have to be before I can drive the tractor by myself?" asked Jean-Claude.

"Not much bigger," said his father encouragingly. "If you are so interested in it, it will be safer if I teach you how to drive it properly. After all, the booklet said that even a child could run it."

Every day Jean-Claude ran across the road to his grandparents' house to make sure that they were really there and that he hadn't dreamed their return.

When he finished helping Papa oil the tractor one day, he set out for the house across the road. Pepère was not in the mill. He was in the shed currying La Blanchet's brown coat. Pepère patted the horse affectionately.

"Ah, my faithful beast," he said, "soon you will not be bored anymore. The wind will be blowing and the mill will be rolling, and you will be walking the mill round from time to time.

Jean-Claude patted the horse too. "It's a good thing Papa didn't sell her," he said.

Pepère stopped currying to look at him. "Your father was going to sell my horse?" he asked.

Jean-Claude had a feeling that he had stepped on unsafe ground. He carefully went over his words in his head before he said them. "That's because he thought you weren't coming back," he explained.

"But why sell La Blanchet even if we didn't return?" asked Pepère. "We often use them as a team. La Blanchet has always pulled well with Jeanette."

"He was going to sell Jeanette too," said Jean-Claude.

"Sell his horse?" asked Pepère. "A man can't farm without horses."

Pepère looked worried. Jean-Claude felt that he had already said too much, so he fell silent as he ran his hand over La Blanchet's smooth side.

After the horse had been curried sleekly as a piece of silk, Pepère went into the house with Jean-Claude at his heels.

"Annik," he called his wife from the kitchen door. "Come here. It is important."

Memère came in from the backyard with a basket of the apples that made such good jelly.

"What is it?" she asked.

"Annik," said Pepère, "I have just found out from Jean-Claude that our son is thinking of selling his animals."

Jean-Claude began to feel uneasy.

"He must need money," said Memère. "It is a good thing I sold my house so that we can help them."

"I remember now that the day we arrived home, he seemed worried about something," said Pepère.

"Yes, I remember too," agreed Memère. "He seemed to have some problem on his mind."

Pepère put his hand on Jean-Claude's shoulder. "Look me between my two eyes, my little goodman, and tell me the truth," he said to the boy. "Does your father need money?"

"Yes," answered Jean-Claude truthfully. "He said that soon he will have nothing but the devil left in his purse."

"I can't understand how a farmer could get hard up so fast," puzzled Pepère. "We have been gone only a few months. It takes years of poor crops to break a farmer."

"Has there been any sickness?" Memère asked Jean-Claude. "Any accidents? Doctor bills?"

"Oh, no," said Jean-Claude, "I didn't hurt myself at all when I ran the tractor into the wall. It was—." The boy clamped his teeth together too late. He had already let the secret out—like the time the mean sow had slipped through the gate even though Papa had tried to open it so carefully.

Pepère slowly took his pipe out of his pocket. He struck a match and tried to light it. Jean-Claude thought that he would never get the pipe going.

"So that is it," said Pepère, blowing a ghost of smoke into the air. "Your father is not poor. He has bought a gasoline machine."

Jean-Claude dumbly nodded his head. There was no use in trying to get this pig back into the pen.

"Better progress than poverty," said Memère in a relieved voice.

Pepère paid no attention to her. He sat down in the rocking chair and sucked at his pipe. "So he did not heed my advice," he said, "because I am old and foolish and have no sense."

"He didn't say that," put in Jean-Claude quickly.

But Memère felt differently. "Perhaps you are," she said tartly to her husband, "but I really think it is none of your business."

Pepère gave her a shocked look. "None of my business!"

he exclaimed. "None of my business that our son has no respect for me? None of my business that my own son thinks me a stupid, old simpleton."

"He didn't say that at all," cried Jean-Claude desperately.

"You are the one saying it," Memère reminded him.

Jean-Claude was terrified. *Aie,* what a storm he had brewed.

"Jean-Claude," said his grandfather, "you will please take a message from me to my son. You will please tell him that he *is* my son so he is always welcome in my house. But you will please tell him that I well never again enter his since he thinks I am foolish with age."

Jean-Claude was only too glad to get away from the trouble he had started at his grandparents' house. But he was not happy with the message he had to deliver.

Papa was splitting some kindling near the woodpile. Jean-Claude especially hated to give such a message to Papa when he was so close to the woodpile.

"Papa," he began, "Pepère said to tell you he is never coming inside our house again."

Papa rested the hatchet. He couldn't understand the

words at first. Jean-Claude tried again. "He is mad at you," he said.

"Mad at me?" asked Papa. "Why?"

"Because you think he is old and foolish," explained Jean-Claude.

Papa threw the hatchet aside. "Jean-Claude," he asked suspiciously, "how could he ever think such a thing? Surely you didn't tell him that. I would never say such a thing about my father."

"No, Papa." Jean-Claude sighed. "I told him something worse. I told him that you have the tractor."

Papa stamped his foot and his black mustache twitched. "Jean-Claude," he roared, "do you dare to stand there and tell me that you told him about the tractor when I distinctly warned you against it?"

Jean-Claude's lower lip began to quiver. "I didn't mean to do it, Papa," he quavered. "It slipped out like that time you let the pig loose even when you tried not to open the gate too wide."

Papa picked up the hatchet and drove its blade into the chopping block. "I will go over there immediately and explain," he said. "I should have done it before."

"May I go too?" begged Jean-Claude.

"Indeed no," cried his father. "You have gone over there once too often already."

So Jean-Claude waited at the foot of the lane. He waited for his father to return. He hoped Papa would make everything all right. It would be a terrible thing if Pepère never entered their house again. He would never have Sunday dinner with them or see Bébé trying to sit up all by herself in her cradle. Not unless they moved the furniture out on the porch.

Jean-Claude felt he had waited days and days for Papa, although the sun wasn't much lower over the St. Lawrence. At last Papa returned, and each step he took dug into the ground.

"My father is as stubborn as his Blanchet," fumed Papa. "He is old and foolish. Never again will I set these feet inside his house. And I don't care a drumbeat whether he enters mine or not."

Jean-Claude felt as if the sun had fallen into the river, putting out its lamp forever. Everything was ruined. The Plouffe family was divided. It was as if the little wooden figures had been separated into two groups.

The river tides rose and fell with the ocean tides. The days went by, but still Pepère and Papa each kept his word.

When they met on the road or in the village, they spoke so politely to each other that a stranger would have thought they were not even cousins. It saddened Jean-Claude to see his grandfather and his father so polite to each other.

But Memère came to see them almost every day. "If he is so childish, let him sit in the corner and suck his thumb," she said of Pepère.

"If only we hadn't bought the tractor," said Maman.

"And why shouldn't you have a tractor," demanded Memère. "It is your money and your business."

So it went and soon the potato harvest began with the red tractor digging up the potatoes and pulling loads of them from the field.

"Next year I will clear some of that wooded land and put in more potatoes," said Papa. "With the tractor, I can take care of another field."

Jean-Claude tried to think of how he could bring a reunion in the Plouffe family and put the little wooden figures into one group again.

Perhaps if he would become a miller instead of a farmer, Pepère would be satisfied. Perhaps he wouldn't be mad at Papa anymore. Jean-Claude remembered how hurt Pepère had been that day in the mill when he had said he wanted to be a farmer with a tractor instead of a miller when he grew up.

Jean-Claude thought of this one day soon after school began. He really should have been studying his spelling, but he kept thinking about the trouble that divided his family.

It was such a windy day that even as he sat inside the schoolroom, Jean-Claude knew the mill must be rolling. Pepère was not one to waste the wind.

The boy was right. As he struggled home with the wind

tearing at his collar, he could see that the arms of the mill were whirling around. Now was the time to tell Pepère that he would become a miller. They would be partners. That would make his grandfather happy. It should make him forgive Papa for buying the tractor. It should unite the family again.

Pepère was glad to see Jean-Claude. He stopped the mill while the boy told him of his decision. Pepère really was pleased.

"And I want to begin being your partner right now," said Jean-Claude. "And Mich' can have the farm and the tractor when he gets big. He can get dressed up and go with Papa across the channel to sign the papers."

He felt as if he were giving away his alder flute, his skates, his wagon and all the things he loved. But he didn't mind because Pepère looked so happy.

Pepère held out his flour-dusted hand and gravely shook hands with his grandson, as if they had signed a paper about it.

"I guess you'll come over to see me soon," added Jean-Claude, "now that we're partners. I guess you'll want to come over and tell Papa and Maman about it. Sometimes they don't listen to me when I talk because they think it isn't important."

Pepère set his jaw. He made no promise and quickly changed the subject.

"That rope has frayed loose," he pointed up the shaft, "and part of it may catch in the cogs. I will have to climb up and break it off."

He carried the ladder over. Jean-Claude helped him brace it against the shaft. "I'll climb up and fix it, Pepère," he said eagerly. "I should learn how to do such things if I am going to be a miller."

To humor him, Pepère held the ladder steady while Jean-Claude climbed it. "You can try," said Pepère, "but maybe I will have to do it."

Jean-Claude climbed within reach of the frayed rope. He pulled at the loose strand. It wouldn't break off. He pulled harder because he wanted to show Pepère that he could do it. In desperation, he gave such a yank that he lost his balance. He clung to the strand with both hands. Then the contrary thing broke loose, and Jean-Claude went tumbling down with the rope in his hands. His head struck the ladder. He lay very still on the floor, like a bag of grain tossed aside. He lay so still because everything inside his well-made head had turned black.

When Jean-Claude awoke from his fall, he didn't know

where he was or what he was for a few seconds. He felt as if he were rising from the bottom of a dark pot. He felt as if he were being stirred by a giant spoon. Perhaps Maman was making soup and he was the beef bone.

No, Maman wasn't stirring him and he wasn't the bone in a soup kettle. He was Jean-Claude Plouffe. He was in Memère's bed and all the family were around him, all but Michel. Even Papa was in Pepère's house.

He must have been stung by the hornets because he could remember reaching for something high above his head. He sat up in the bed and asked, "What happened to the hornets' nest?"

Maman burst into tears.

"He is out of his mind," she cried. "I do hope Michel will hurry with the priest and the doctor."

Suddenly a light was turned on in Jean-Claude's head. "I remember now," he said. "I climbed up the ladder to tear the piece of frayed rope away."

Maman felt the bump on his head. "It is big as a potato," she said.

"I think he is himself again," said Papa.

"How do you feel?" asked Memère.

Jean-Claude slowly broke away from their arms and stood up. He didn't feel dizzy and he didn't fall over. "We must go back and fix the rope, Pepère," he said. "This time I will let you do it."

Pepère wiped his eyes and shook his lynx whiskers. "No, my little goodman," he said. "My mill and I are getting too old to work. Even on Ré, they have stopped using the mills. From now on we will take it easy and enjoy the new times."

"But the tractor," said Jean-Claude. "The tractor belongs to the new times."

"So it does," said Pepère, "and so do you, my little goodman. You must grow up and be a new-style farmer. If you feel well enough now, we will walk over to your house so I can see this new-fashioned gasoline machine."

Jean-Claude felt well enough. Despite the potato on his head, he had never felt better in his life.

They all left the bedroom and went out of the house. They walked down Pepère's lane with Jean-Claude between his grandparents, holding a hand of each.

"The priest," remembered Maman. "The doctor can look over Jean-Claude to see that he is really all right, but what about the priest?"

"Let him come," said Papa. "We shall have him bless the tractor. If we had had it blessed at the very beginning, it might not have caused so much trouble."

Jean-Claude felt so well that he couldn't walk as slowly

as Memère and Pepère. He let go of their hands and went skipping ahead. He turned two cartwheels into the wind. He raised his arms like a bird and made little leaps into the air. He was so happy that he belonged to the Plouffe family.

Format by Gertrude Awe
Set in Linotype Caslon
Composed and bound by The Haddon Craftsmen, Inc.
Printed by The Murray Printing Co.
HARPER & ROW, PUBLISHERS, INCORPORATED